# WHOSE AFRAID OF THE GHOST?

The roaring sound dimmed as the whirlwind stopped moving and everything crammed together. Mitzi wasn't happy. She shrieked. A demonic sound that sent prickles of ice down my spine. She fought hard, and I wound my magic around the entire mess, deciding overkill was the better part of glory, not to mention survival.

I contemplated the hovering mess, trying to decide what to do next. I needed to extract Mitzi and then set all the rest of the crap on the floor, though I doubted enough survived for a decent sale. Apparently, Mitzi didn't like her daughters consorting with their enemy cousin and planning to make Lindsey part-owner of the new business.

A shiver ran through me, and a droplet of cold water landed on my forehead. I looked up to the ceiling. Melting icicles hung like stalactites from the chandeliers.

Abruptly the shrieking cut off. My stomach curled.

That couldn't be good.

# PUTTING THE CHIC IN PSYCHIC

## EVERYDAY DISASTERS BOOK 2

### DIANA PHARAOH FRANCIS

*PUTTING THE CHIC IN PSYCHIC*
*Everyday Disasters: Book 2*
Diana Pharaoh Francis
Copyright 2022 by Diana Pharaoh Francis
ISBN 978-1-944756-06-2
Published by Book View Café in conjunction with Lucky Foot Press 2023
Originally published in *Dirty Deeds II*, Pen & Page Publishing, 2022

PRODUCTION TEAM:
Cover illustration and design by Lyn Forester
Copyediting and proofreading by Patricia Rice
Ebook design and formatting by Jennifer Stevenson
Print design and formatting by Diana Pharaoh Francis



Lucky Foot Press
*in conjunction with*
Book View Café
304 S. Jones Blvd. Suite #2906
Las Vegas NV 89107
www.bookviewcafe.com

BOOK VIEW CAFE

# MORE BOOKS BY DIANA PHARAOH FRANCIS

From Book View Café and Lucky Foot Press

EVERYDAY DISASTERS

*Putting the Fun in Funeral*

*Putting the Chic in Psychic*

*Putting the Ice in Nice* (Forthcoming)

MISSION: MAGIC

*The Incubus Trap* (Forthcoming)

*The Elf Deception* (Forthcoming)

*The Giant Riot* (Forthcoming)

THE PATH SERIES

*Path of Fate* (Forthcoming)

*Path of Honor* (Forthcoming)

*Path of Blood* (Forthcoming)

*The Quick and Dirty Guide to Character Creation* (Forthcoming)

Books from Other Publishers

Diamond City Magic series

*Trace of Magic*

*Edge of Dreams*

*Whisper of Shadows*

*Shades of Memory*

*Shatter of Light*

Crosspointe Chronicles

*The Cipher*

*The Black Ship*

*The Turning Tide*

*The Hollow Crown*

Horngate Witches series

*Bitter Night*

*Crimson Wind*

*Shadow City*

*Blood Winter*

Magicfall series

*The Witchkin Murders*

*For Tony, the love of my life.*

# CHAPTER ONE

I couldn't deny I was having a damned good start to the day. My fake mother—aka Aunty Mommy—remained dead and had thus far been unable to rise from the grave and haunt me; my savagely vandalized business was under reconstruction; nobody had tried to kill me recently; my dog, Ajax, loved me unconditionally, as did my three best friends; and I was enjoying the nectar of the gods—aka an extra large 9-1-1 espresso—with a gorgeous man.

Yeah, maybe I had a few problems, but at the moment, I could ignore all of them and enjoy the lovely weather and the very fine specimen of masculinity sitting across from me.

I sipped my ultra-caffeinated brew, eyeing Damon over the rim of my cup. He was flat out hot. Like HAWT. I'd seen him mostly naked and could attest to six pack abs, broad shoulders, and thighs that could crack walnuts. And his ass. It could make a nun wet her panties. With that body, his dark blond hair, stormy blue eyes, and chiseled jaw, he could have been a model. The fact that he was eyeing me with the same orgasmic appreciation I'd just given the first sip of my coffee made me want to lick him like a lollipop.

Just at the moment, my life was closer to perfect than it had ever been, which of course meant that everything would shortly be going straight to hell. Murphy's Law and Mercury in Retrograde are the ruling forces of my life. Trouble was always lying in wait just around the corner. At least it meant life was exciting. Often hideously painful, but still exciting. It also meant I knew enough to enjoy the good while it lasted.

I am an almost twenty-eight-year-old business woman and witch. I run Effortless Estates, a high-end estate liquidation business. I hold wealthy estate sales and have a showroom of the more valuable pieces. Or I did, before a former colleague destroyed it out of frustration, all because I refused to die when he was trying to murder me. Luckily he did succeed in offing Aunty Mommy, which made me almost willing to forgive him for my attempted murder, except he'd also tried to kill my three BFFs—Stacey, Jen, and Lorraine—not to mention Damon and my recently discovered uncle.

Nobody fucks with the people I love and gets away with it. Nobody.

Anyhow, my business had really taken off in the last few years, growing like a weed on steroids. Damon's a lawyer. My lawyer, as of recently. I'm his only client. When Aunty Mommy kicked the bucket, all sorts of cockroaches crawled out of the woodwork, including my real parents and a bunch of other family, also all witches. I'd learned I was the product of a birth contract, and that the entire witch world revolved around bloodlines and eugenics, and my eggs were in high demand. All of which was enough to make me throw up in my mouth.

But I also inherited a convoluted mess of money and property, and Damon had taken on untangling and managing it all, so I wouldn't have to. If I'd had my way, I'd have refused to take it. I considered it blood money—specifically *my* blood—but I had to be practical, one of my least favorite things to be when I was pissed off. It turned out I wasn't the only target of Aunty Mommy's, just her favorite. She'd been a category nine tornado and had left a whole lot of damage in her wake. Since nobody else would, I had to try to fix what I could, and that meant money and plenty of it.

Between the convoluted finances, the fact that I'd never been trained in magic, my current lack of a home (my ex-colleague had destroyed my apartment along with my showroom), Damon and I were practically glued together these days. He was super protective of me, and though he hadn't said much, I knew he was scared some witch family —or just as likely my own—would kidnap me and turn me into an Easy-bake Oven for magically powerful babies. He'd been giving me a crash course in witchcraft. Not that I didn't have good command of my power—I did. I just didn't know how to create spells or what ingredients to use for what, nor did I really know the dangers, or even what I could or should be doing to protect myself. Other than that, I was in good shape.

His concern and me being his only client made it hard for him to peel away from me, which was both flattering to my female sensibilities and annoying as fuck. I didn't need him underfoot twenty-four/seven, no matter how pretty he was, or how much I enjoyed his company. The constant togetherness had started to feel claustrophobic, which could be totally normal, or could be me panicking over being in a relationship.

Just at the moment, however, everything gleamed shiny perfection.

"What are your plans for the day?" He asked, interrupting my rambling train of thought.

"I'm going to check on the construction progress, and I have a couple potential clients to meet with about sales this weekend. Later, I'm having dinner with the girls. What about you?"

"More of the same. Sorting out your aunt's financial estate. It's like picking apart a gordian knot."

"Sounds horrifying."

The corners of his mouth kicked up. "I enjoy puzzles. There's no satisfaction like solving a difficult one."

"I like puzzles just fine, but that mess is sheer torture."

"Which is why you have me to sort it out for you."

"Lighting it on fire would be more satisfying."

"But far less profitable. Anyway, you can bask in the knowledge that your aunt would have hated knowing that you are the sole beneficiary of her financial empire. Milking it for all it's worth is the best sort of revenge."

"I don't know. Peeing on her grave felt pretty good. The girls and I plan to make it a regular thing. Weekly maybe."

"I'll keep bail money on hand. Just in case you get caught."

He smirked, unfazed by the idea of me, Jen, Stacey, and Lorraine out in the cemetery and squatting on Aunty Mommy's grave. Chalk up another reason to keep him around.

"Have you thought any more about what you want to do with the estate?"

"Much as I'd like to burn it to the ground, Mason is right. Until I can free the gargoyles, I have to keep it. I don't suppose there's any way to curse Aunty Mommy, is there?"

Damon shook his head. "There's no reaching across the veil, I'm afraid."

"Karma has seriously let me down. I hope there's a hell, and she's burning in it," I complained.

He lost his smile, his gaze turning dark. He still hadn't come to terms with the things my aunt had done to me. Not that we talked about it. As far as I was concerned, that part of my life lived behind a locked door, and I was never opening it again. Out of sight, out of mind. As a coping mechanism, it worked most of the time. Like when I was awake.

"Believe me, if there was a way to get at the bitch, I would already have done it," he said in a stone voice.

"I know. And I appreciate it." I stroked my fingers over the back of his hand. He grasped mine. "The idea of making the estate a sanctuary appeals a lot to me," I said, returning to the subject at hand. "Lorraine could potentially move her vet clinic there and focus more on rescues if she wants, and I could fund the whole shebang. I've got to talk to the gargoyles, though. The place is their home more than mine, and they deserve the deciding vote on what happens there."

He nodded. "They will appreciate your consideration."

I shrugged. "It's the right thing to do."

"For you. Many would disagree."

"Apparently, many are psychopaths, then."

"Agreed."

Just then, his phone bleeped with a text notification. He glanced at it and his expression darkened. His jaw knotted. "Excuse me a minute," he said. "This can't wait."

I watched him stalk away, lifting his phone to his ear. Damon's entire body radiated tension. Foreboding stirred in my gut, an all too familiar feeling.

I drew a slow breath and let it go, trying to relax. No

good. My rational brain had lost all control, and my primal self had taken over. A life of constant threat combined with endless torture had honed my survival instincts. It didn't matter how nebulous my uneasiness was, or that I had no good reason to think trouble was on its way. Primitive me had decided to circle the wagons, raise all the drawbridges, and load all the weapons. In the space of a few seconds, the new, defenselessly happy me vanished and the old me—scarred, jaded, and suspicious—returned.

In an effort to distract myself, I sent a couple of work texts while keeping a covert eye on Damon. He'd begun to pace, his free hand balled into a fist. Ajax, my wolf-dog, made a protesting sound, his ears pricked like little satellite dishes as he also watched Damon.

I stroked his head, infusing my voice with a calm I didn't feel. "Easy now. Everything's okay."

He visibly relaxed, and he looked up at me, his light brown eyes softening. He rolled onto his side so I could scratch his stomach. I obliged with a little chuckle. His eyes drifted shut.

Ever since I'd helped Lorraine rescue him, he and I had pretty much been inseparable. He'd become just as much family to me as Jen, Stacey, and Lorraine. Luckily Damon didn't mind sharing the bed with both of us, as Ajax tended to want to snuggle at night.

I smiled to myself. Even if Damon did mind, he'd have to get over it. Though how we were going to manage to have sex—if and when that time came—I didn't know. I didn't want an audience, furry or otherwise, and if we locked him in another room, I don't know if Ajax would rip down the wall, thinking I was under attack or something.

I planned to be a noisy lover.

"Something funny?" Damon returned to the table. He

didn't sit down, and his dark expression was the polar opposite of his lightly spoken question.

"What's going on? You look pissed, and I want to note for the record, this time it wasn't me."

He didn't even crack the slightest smile. I wasn't sure he even heard me. He was tapping out a text. "Problems at home. I've got to fly back, and I don't know how long I'll be gone."

I hadn't known Damon long. A few months is all, and he'd seen me through some near-death experiences, so we'd bonded pretty quickly. Enough that he'd told me he loved me a few weeks into our acquaintance, plus invited me to live with him while my loft was getting rebuilt.

I'd begun to think of him as a fixture in my life, as reliable as the ground or the air, so with that kind of news, I naturally expected to anticipate missing him. What I didn't anticipate was the shaft of hurt that stabbed through me, threatening to double me over. For a second I couldn't even move.

*Problems at home.* The phrase rattled around in my skull like a pinball in a clothes dryer. Because his home was not here. It hadn't occurred to me that he'd leave eventually, and I wasn't prepared for the idea.

*He just said he didn't know how long he'd be gone,* I reminded myself. *He's planning to come back. He's been looking at real estate so he can move his ass here. Besides, you've been whining about having some time to yourself. Now you get to have it, so quit being such a baby.*

Oh, for fuck's sake. I was reading way too much into the situation. I was a walking soap opera, not to mention a complete nutcase.

I decided that silence was the best way not to make a total ass of myself. I got up and disposed of our garbage.

Damon was still tapping away on his phone as we started back toward the hotel. He fell in beside me, barely looking up from his screen. Since he was in a hurry, I kept a brisk pace, Ajax trotting happily beside me.

I'd already decided I didn't want to figure out new doubts to torture myself with while Damon packed. As we approached the elegant boutique hotel where we'd been living, I slowed. "I'm just going to head out." I nudged my chin toward the entrance to the parking garage. "You don't need a ride to the airport, do you?"

He tore himself away from his phone long enough to glance at me. "No. I'll have the hotel shuttle take me."

Shuttle. As if. It was a limo.

"Well, have a good trip. Hope everything's okay." I winced. Lame. Could I have come up with anything more impersonal? Maybe if I'd said Dear Sir or Madam at the beginning. Or To Whom It May Concern.

His attention had returned to his phone, and he didn't seem to notice my awkwardness.

"Everything will be fine," he said.

"I guess I'll see you when I see you then," I said, uncertain whether I should interrupt his focus for a kiss goodbye. I waited a few seconds for him to say or do something, but it appeared he'd forgotten me. I gave a little shrug and left, squelching my hurt and self pity. Damon wasn't given to hysterics, so whatever was going on had to be pretty bad. The situation wasn't about me at all, so I just needed to get over myself.

I waved at Josef, who was currently alone at the valet stand, and kept going, the cool, dark air of the garage closing around me. They'd long ago gotten used to me parking and unparking my own car, back when it was a gorgeous classic Thunderbird in near mint condition. But then the attack on my business had happened, and the Thunderbird had been a casualty. I hadn't decided yet if I wanted to use magic to fix it. Garrett Sandrini, a secret witch and my would-be murderer, had chopped it in half long ways. Fixing it using ordinary methods wouldn't be feasible.

Every time I thought of replacing it, I felt guilty, like I was betraying it. I'd been contemplating using magic to fix it but change the paint and interior colors. Then I could claim it was a different vehicle altogether.

I sighed. Stupid to get so upset about a car. I should just suck it up and find something else. Maybe a Ranchero or an El Camino. Or a Mustang fastback. Anything but the Toyota Highlander I'd been renting. Though to be fair, it was nice enough and had a lot of room for all the things I had to carry to and from sales. It just didn't have much by way of charm, not like a classic car.

I'd walked down the ramp to the second level when I heard rapid footsteps behind me.

"Beck, wait."

I stopped and waited for Damon to approach. His brow was furrowed, and his jaw looked like it was sculpted from granite.

"What's up?"

He grimaced. "I'm sorry."

"For what?" I was acting a little too innocent, but I didn't want him to know I'd been hurt.

"For being a dick to you."

"You weren't a dick," I said. Okay, maybe a little bit, but I was frequently a bitch and a half, so I couldn't very well complain.

He raised his brows in clear disbelief. "I was, and I'm concerned that you aren't calling me on it."

I shrugged. "Whatever you have to deal with is clearly upsetting you. I don't need to make it any worse."

He tipped his head, his eyes narrowing. "That's very adult of you."

"Now you're being rude."

"I was rude outside, but that didn't seem to bother you."

"And what should I have said? Don't ignore me? Don't shut me out? Who am I to make those kinds of demands? Anyhow, it's clearly none of my business."

His mouth tightened and his eyes flashed with fury. "Is that what you really think?"

"I think if it were my business, you'd talk to me about it. You haven't, so..." I shrugged again. I knew I was pissing him off. I knew I sounded like a grade A super bitch. At least I was an elite bitch and not middle-of-the-road or mediocre. I probably shouldn't have taken pride in that, but gotta take credit where credit is due.

His jaw knotted, and I could practically see steam rising from the top of his head. I tried to feel sorry about that, but I couldn't. Riling him up meant he wasn't ignoring me any more. So much for being an adult.

"It's family business," he said in a clipped voice.

"Okay."

"I have to go help sort it out."

"You said that."

"I don't *want* to go, but I don't have a choice."

Well, if that wasn't mysterious, I didn't know what was. "Okay," I said again. I wondered if he noticed he hadn't offered any details. Whether he meant to or not, he *was* shutting me out.

"Could you maybe say something more than just okay?" He growled.

"Like what?"

"Maybe that you'll miss me? You don't want me to go? Anything besides the cold fish act?"

"I *will* miss you," I said. "And I don't particularly want you to go."

"But?"

"But nothing."

He glared. "Talking to you is like trying to get gold out of Fort Knox. Sometimes I wonder if you're a robot."

My teeth clenched together. And here I thought we'd been getting along. I stepped back so that I wouldn't slug him. "You're going to miss your flight."

"That's it? That's all you have to say?"

I considered him as I tried to formulate what I wanted to say. I edited out the *fuck you, asshole* part. "I think," I said instead, "that this is probably a stupid argument that's quickly going way off the rails. Whatever is wrong, you clearly need to go handle it. I'll be here when you get back, and we can fight about something stupid then, if you still want to. In the meantime..." I closed the space between us and put my arms around his waist. See? I can adult.

He snatched me close and nuzzled my hair as I pressed my face into his chest and drew a deep breath. He smelled of himself, fresh air, and the spicy soap he used. It made me want to rub all over him like a cat.

"Christ, but I don't want to leave you," he muttered in a gravelly voice.

"I'd go with you, but I have too much to do."

I felt him shake his head. "Last thing I want is to take you back there."

I pushed back, looking up at him. "My manners aren't *that* bad," I said. "I rarely ever pee on the furniture or chew shoes anymore. And I know how to use *all* the silverware."

A smile ghosted over his lips before he sobered again. "It's too dangerous. You're a golden goose, remember? Too many will want to scoop you up and use you to breed the Osterraven and Wyler Simms magic genetics into their families."

I rolled my eyes. The witch world's fucked up eugenics program was the whole reason I existed.

"I'm not going to let anybody scoop me up."

He shook his head. "You're powerful, but you won't stand a chance if someone organizes a plot to grab you. At least here you stand a better chance of seeing trouble coming, and if need be, you can take refuge at the estate. The gargoyles will protect you."

"Because they don't have a choice. I'm not going to take advantage of them."

"They won't mind. You're working on freeing them. They want you safe."

I looked away. I had no intention of using the gargoyles like that. He cupped my cheek and pulled me back around until I met his gaze.

"Promise me you'll go to them for help if you need it."

"I guess," I agreed reluctantly. "*If* I need it."

He didn't look entirely satisfied but nodded. "Good. Are you going to tell me what's bothering you?"

Crap. He had the memory of an elephant sometimes. I looked away again. "It's stupid and not worth talking about, especially when you're in a hurry."

Once again he made me look at him. "Nothing between us is stupid, and everything about you is worth talking about. I'm never too much in a hurry to make sure things are good between us."

"That's sappy," I said, even though warm pleasure

washed through me. "Have you been watching the Hallmark Channel again?"

"I meant every word. Tell me what's wrong." His gaze locked mine in place.

I sighed. "You said you were going home."

He waited for more, his brow furrowing as I remained silent.

"See? I told you it was stupid," I said, starting to pull away. He clamped his hands tighter.

I could practically see his mind spinning in high gear as he tried to sort the puzzle out. Realization lit his expression after a moment, and he looked pleased.

"You're pissed because you don't want me to go," he said smugly and then kissed me before I could reply.

I'm not ashamed to say I melted. His touch had that effect on me. Sizzling fireworks burst in my chest and hunger dug its claws into me. In a matter of a millisecond I went from normal temperature to conflagration, and I didn't mind a bit.

Damon was a good kisser, at least according to my limited experience. He speared his fingers through my hair and cupped my head. His other hand pressed me closer. Tingles of desire sparked across my skin, and I made a sound. Could have been a moan, could have been a whimper, could have been a demand for more. Maybe it was all three. At any rate, I wanted more.

In response, Damon hitched me closer, pulling me up on tiptoe. The hand holding my head slid down to cup my ass, while the other one worked upward to brush against the outer curve of my mashed breasts. The sensations made me crazy, and I couldn't help rubbing my aching lady-bits against his male hardness.

He made a primal sound deep in his throat and lifted

his head. "I want you so goddamn bad." He brushed a thumb over my lips. "I love the way you look when I touch you. Like you got hit with a sledgehammer. I can't wait to see how you'll look when I'm inside you."

I wanted to protest his assumption that it was 'when' and not 'if,' but I didn't have a leg to stand on. Right at the moment, I was more than ready to go upstairs and find out what I'd been missing. Then his words caught up with me along with the image of us naked and him between my legs, sucking on my breasts, and I just about orgasmed right there. I closed my eyes and pinched my lips together to keep from begging him to stick his hand down my pants to see just how magic his fingers could be.

"Look at me."

I reluctantly obeyed, only to instantly get lost in the stormy depths of his eyes. "Should I be looking for something in particular? A cataract? Maybe a stye?"

He smiled. "Would you please just shut up?"

"Talk about fickle. A minute ago you were demanding I spill my guts. Make up your mind, already."

"Tell me the rest of what's bugging you." His brows rose in challenge.

Dammit. Why did he have to be so smart? "Who said there's anything else?"

"Isn't there?"

I'm not a good liar. I don't generally see the point. Sooner or later the truth will bite you in the ass, so better to deal with it up front. "Maybe." My cheeks heated and flushed. Could my humiliation get much worse?

"Why don't you explain it to me because clearly I don't get it."

"I thought you liked puzzles. Figure it out."

"How can I fix the problem if I don't even know what it is?" he asked, exasperated.

"What makes you think you have to fix anything? It's my problem, *I'll* solve it."

He ran his hands up my arms. "I want you to be happy. Why wouldn't I try to help?"

"Maybe because I'm not a damsel in distress." It came out more sharply than I planned. The fact was, I didn't want to be rescued. I didn't want Damon here because he felt responsible for me.

"I know you don't need a knight in shining armor," he said exasperatedly. "But can't I support you? Help you? Isn't that what... friends... do?"

He hesitated slightly at 'friends' as if that wasn't the word he meant but was afraid to spook me. Was that how he saw me? That I couldn't handle what he really wanted to say? Did he think I'd freak out and run in the other direction?

To be fair, I hadn't given him any reason to think that I wouldn't. As far as he knew, I was only living at the hotel with him out of necessity. My home was trashed, and I hated Aunty Mommy's estate, which was my other option. And the hundreds of other hotel rooms available, not to mention rental apartments and houses, that I could easily afford. None those options seemed to occur to him.

"Are we friends?" I wondered aloud. My reaction when he'd mentioned going home made it crystal clear that I felt a lot more than that. The idea of confessing that to Damon made me nauseous. My entire childhood had revolved around hiding my feelings and trusting only myself, Jen, Lorraine, and Stacey, and as much as I loved them, I kept everything I could hidden. It was a tough habit to break.

"You doubt it?"

The chill in Damon's voice brought me back to the moment. He pushed away, putting a couple feet of space between us. The day was warm, but a shiver swept through me. My careless question had hurt him, and I needed to fix it. I had to stop playing it safe. Anyhow, I'd never let fear of pain be the reason I did anything in my life, and I wasn't going to start now.

"You said you had to go home." I folded my arms over my chest and waited for him to say something, but he remained silent. I swallowed and slogged onward. "You reminded me Sweetwater isn't your home. Your stay is temporary."

Silence fell between us as he processed that. A car door slammed, and voices drifted from further up the ramp. Uncomfortable with his penetrating gaze, I started to babble. I couldn't find the off switch either. Words just kept spewing out, miring me deeper in idiocy.

"I don't even know why I thought you'd be staying. You're living in a hotel. That's the definition of temporary. Your whole life is somewhere else, and you must be getting pretty homesick by now. You've been here weeks and weeks without seeing your family or friends. I hate to imagine the piles of mail you've got waiting. All the food in your refrigerator has probably turned into a science experiment, and you have to be insanely annoyed at having to wear the same clothes over and over. Staying here has put your whole life on hold. You must be dying to get back."

Every sentence added a pebble in my throat, which I could only hope would dam up my verbal diarrhea. Instead, they just made my throat ache. Coincidentally, my eyes started burning, too, as rebellious tears threatened.

I finally resorted to biting my tongue. Hitching my purse higher on my shoulder, I tangled my fingers in Ajax's ruff. He leaned against me, offering comfort. "Anyhow, I should get going. You don't want to be late for your flight. I'll come back later and clear my stuff out of the suite, so you can check out. I can stay with one of the girls."

I hesitated. Should I kiss him goodbye? A peck on the cheek, maybe? Or a hug? Or just go? He seemed disinclined to move. The pebbles in my throat melded into a boulder. Any minute now, I was going to have a royal meltdown with lots of tears and snot. I needed Damon to *not* see that.

I forced a smile. "Okay, so text me when you get a chance and let me know how you are." With that, I spun around and strode away. I made three steps before he spun me back around.

"Text you? Seriously, Beck?"

He didn't sound as annoyed as I probably would have been. In fact he sounded exasperated and maybe a little amused. Not the reaction I was expecting, but I suppose it only reinforced the fact that whatever he thought he felt for me, he also knew it wasn't going anywhere. It occurred to me then that he hadn't told me he loved me since my last near-death debacle. That had to be a sign. Walking the edge of death just to keep the romance going didn't seem all that healthy.

Damon tugged me toward him, but I held myself away, my body stiff. When I wouldn't move, he stepped closer.

"Look at me."

I shook my head and stared at the cinderblock wall. "I'm good."

"I'd really rather not talk to the side of your head."

"Shouldn't you be going to pack? Your trip sounded pretty urgent."

He sighed. "I'm not even going to dignify that with a response."

"That actually counts as a response, so really, you did dignify it. Whatever that means."

"I misspoke."

"That's what I just said."

"I misspoke about the trip. About going home."

I frowned and accidentally looked at him. "How so?"

"Finally."

He captured my face between his palms, so I couldn't turn away. Not that he needed to hold me. The intensity of his gaze fixed me in place. I couldn't have moved if I wanted to. I could hardly even breathe.

"I need you to hear me, Beck. Are you listening?"

"Be hard not to. I'm not deaf."

His mouth curved. "Good. Then understand this. My only home is here, with you. *You* are my home. You're my gravity, the center of my universe. Nothing about me being here is temporary. I'm going to be back here as soon as humanly possible, and while I'm gone, I'm going to be wishing with all my heart I was here. Please don't move out. I don't want to come back to a cold, empty room. I want to think of you sleeping in my bed, in *our* bed, and know you'll be waiting for me when I come back."

My breath caught in my chest. My eyes went so wide I must have looked like I didn't have eyelids, and the tears I'd been keeping at bay overflowed. My heart pounded ninety miles a minute.

Damon's brow creased, and he slid his hands down to my shoulders. "Tears, Beck? You never cry."

That seemed to kick me out of frozen rabbit mode. I rolled my eyes. "Oh, please. Of course I cry. All the time. It's a perfectly normal human response to all sorts of emotions. I'm not a robot, you know." Even though he called me one.

"I know, believe me. Would you mind telling me why you're crying? It's killing me a little."

"I didn't even know you could kill in increments. I thought it was an either/or sort of situation. Sort of like being pregnant."

"Turns out, you can. Are you going to tell me?"

"If I have to."

He waited. "Now?"

"Be patient. It's very confusing. I've never had feelings like this before, and they are a little overwhelming."

His frown smoothed away, and a smile curved his lips. A distinctly relieved smile, with a little smugness thrown in. "Take your time."

"You haven't told me that you love me since we freed the female gargoyles. Combine that with you saying you're going home, and I figured it meant you'd gotten tired and given up on me, or maybe realized I wasn't worth the hassle, or that you'd been mistaken about loving me."

His fingers tightened, and he looked consternated. "I thought if I kept telling you, you'd feel like I was pressuring you. I do love you. That's not ever going to change." He paused. "It bothered you I might not love you?"

I made a face. "Seems like."

"So that means you have feelings for me, too?"

"I've always had feelings for you."

"I was hoping for something better than hate, distrust, dislike, fury, disgust, resentment, annoyance.... I could go on."

I choked out a laugh. "You forgot panty-melting attraction."

"I wasn't aware that your panties had been melting," he said, brows arching. "Tell me more."

"Don't you have a plane to catch? Fires to put out?"

"They'll wait."

"You didn't seem to think so back at the café."

"I was an ignorant idiot at the café. I got over it. Talk to me."

I heave a sigh. "Fine. I have feelings for you. Good feelings," I added. "I'm just not entirely sure what they are. I have zero experience in this arena."

He smoothed a hand over my hair. It felt so good I'd have purred if I could.

"That's really, *really* good to hear. When I come *home*, maybe we can talk about it some more. Help you figure it out."

Or maybe move to the showing part. I'd been holding back because neither one of us were the sort to have casual sex, and I didn't want to hurt Damon by pretending to feel more than I did. Except now I knew I wouldn't be pretending. In fact, I was beginning to think I'd actually fallen in love with him. Or if not, I was on my way.

We should definitely move on to the showing part. I could practically hear Stacey, Lorraine, and Jen squealing and throwing confetti. They thought I should have been riding him like a stallion practically since they'd first seen him.

Nervousness, anticipation, and joy bubbled through me. My smile grew wide enough to cramp my cheeks.

"Sure," I said. "We'll... talk. I can't wait."

# CHAPTER TWO

After saying goodbye to Damon—which involved more mind-blowing kissing and maybe a little under the clothes petting and possibly a hickey or two, not to mention moaning and way too much unresolved aching—I managed to drive myself to my store/home.

Formerly a granary and feed store, I'd turned it into a showroom for pieces that were too good to put estate sale prices on. Besides the showroom, it contained a warehouse, my office, and a garage for my car and the box truck. My apartment took up half of the top floor, and I'd never gotten around to doing anything with the other half.

After Garrett had vandalized the place in a fit of rage, it had needed a lot of rebuilding. Amazing what a pissed off witch can do. Every single window required replacement, all the electric lines, the floors, the sheetrock and a lot of the studs.... Basically a total gut job.

With all the construction going on, I'd put the rest of my employees to work expanding the estate sale side of things, so that we could do multiple sales on any given weekend. I'd been wanting to anyway, and business was booming. I'd rented warehouse space for the pieces that I ordinarily would have put in the showroom, and I'd been shopping them around to my contacts all over the world. I'd also had my website updated with current inventory.

I checked in with Kevin, my manager, and spent a couple hours touring the site, talking to the contractor, and going over orders for fixtures, lights, floors, tile, cabinets, knobs, and a million other things. I was getting ready to break for lunch when a gold Porsche convertible drove into the parking lot. The top was down, but not one strand of the driver's hair was out of place. Magic, I supposed, watching her park sideways of the lines and taking up three spots. If my mother was trying to make a good impression, she was off to a bad start.

She waved vigorously at me, the faceted stones in her chunky gold bracelet flashing in the sunlight. She wore big sunglasses, a green designer dress that screamed wealth and elegance, and high heels with what I assumed were real emeralds scattered carelessly across the leather.

She hurried across the pavement to where I stood beside my very ordinary and practical car.

"Rebecca, I'm so glad I caught you."

Made one of us. I barely kept myself from saying it. Elena Wyler Symms looked a little too much like her sister —Aunty Mommy—and I couldn't help the flash of knee-jerk hatred I felt every time I saw her. It wasn't her fault and not fair to hold her responsible. She'd been tricked into gestating me, and then Aunty Mommy had kidnapped me. Nothing was her fault.

She also looked a lot like me. Or I looked like her. Whatever. She had an oval face with honey-colored hair that nearly matched mine, except she'd probably dropped a thousand dollars or more on her chic hair style.

"Call me Beck," I said yet again. I don't know how many times I'd told her.

She gave it a little pout. She was way too fucking old to pout. "But Rebecca is such a lovely name."

"I hate the name, and it's rude to continue to use it when I've asked you not to."

Her eyes widened. "I didn't realize you find it so offensive." A note of haughtiness tinged the not-quite-an-apology.

"Now you do. Did you get a new car?"

"I wanted a convertible. Do you like it?"

"It's pretty." I just preferred classic cars, and the Porsche was a little ostentatious. "What brings you by?"

"I wanted to invite you to dinner tonight. Are you free? I'll invite Mason, and you can bring Mister Matrovani. We haven't had a chance to spend much time together."

She sounded wistful and there was a sadness lurking in her eyes that made me want to say yes. She came from the world of witches, which was a world of wealth and power, but also one of insanity, if you asked me. All the children had to participate in the whole eugenics program. Families contracted pregnancies, breeding for power. The children were disseminated according to the contractual dictates, and the other parent's family had nothing to do with them.

Ethan Osterraven, my sperm donor, wanted to use me the same way. I'd told the bastard he could take his demands and go fuck himself with them, but I doubted he'd given up on me. Or rather, my uterus, because really, what else could possibly matter? That was one of Damon's fears: that good ole dad planned to snatch me, and if not him, another baby-hungry family.

"I've got plans already," I said. "We could meet up for lunch tomorrow if you like."

Disappointment dimmed her enthusiasm. "I wanted to have you over to my new house. It's quite lovely."

Surprise of a not particularly pleasant variety widened my eyes. "That was quick."

She waved a dismissive hand. "I paid cash with inducements to vacate immediately, and had my decorator renovate. He's from the Medevec family and has stellar taste. I left everything in his hands, and he and his people worked around the clock to get everything in order. It didn't take long at all. They put in a gorgeous pool with waterfalls and a lazy river. It's almost as big as the house."

"Sounds impressive," I said dryly. I had no doubt they'd used a hefty load of magic to make the renovations happen too quickly.

"I flew the staff in from my other homes. They all have minor magical talents, which they put to excellent use in domestic work. My chef is utterly divine. His bluefin tuna with white truffles is a taste of paradise." She hesitated. "I hoped to make a place you'd want to visit. We haven't really talked much since..." She trailed off, turning her sparkling bracelet around her wrist.

"Why do you want to know me?" The question had been gnawing at me. Damon's suspicion of her motivations only increased my own.

"You're my daughter."

I shrugged. "You have other kids and didn't raise them either. So what makes my disappearance such a big deal to you? I wasn't even part of the contract. You can't miss what you didn't even know you lost, and even if you'd known about me, I'd have gone to my father per the contract. I don't buy that you have an abiding love for me. It makes a lot more sense if you're out to convince me to return to the family fold and make babies, or maybe you just plan to kidnap me."

I studied her as I spoke, trying to get a bead on what she was really thinking. She flushed, and her back stiffened at my accusations, but instead of an angry retort, she averted her eyes as if embarrassed.

"I don't remember giving birth. I was sick for weeks after, and no magic seemed to help. They even tried ordinary medicine. Eventually I recovered, but I had postpartum depression. They medicated me and told me to get over it. They said I was lucky and should be grateful. I didn't feel lucky."

"I couldn't seem to stop crying or stop wanting you— all three of you. I've never even met your brother or sister. Ethan keeps them on a tight leash. Not that they'd be interested in knowing me. I never had more children. I couldn't bear it. Nor did I want to raise any of the children from other family contracts. Mostly I wanted to disappear."

The rawness of her emotion saturated the words. I had no doubt she spoke the truth. You just couldn't fake that kind of pain.

She looked at me, her eyes haunted. "I did all the things I was supposed to do. I studied and got a degree, and I went to work. I kept myself busy with all sorts of unimportant activities that I couldn't really care about. When I learned you were alive, it's like color came back to my world. I dropped everything and came as fast as I could. I was terrified Ethan would drag you away before I could even meet you." A smile curved her lips. "I imagine you gave him quite a shock when you refused to have anything to do with him."

"He did seem startled," I acknowledged.

"Beck, I know my sister abused you, and I don't want to make your life difficult. All I want is to get to know you. I bought the house in the hopes you'd want to spend time there, and so you'd know I'm sincere and committed to doing whatever I need to do. You might not be ready to have me in your life, but maybe one day you will be. When that happens, I'm going to be here, waiting."

The whole confession was heartbreaking, but her last words kicked me in the gut. I knew exactly how she felt. The longing for someone to care about you and knowing it might never happen. When I was little and still hadn't figured out how much Aunty Mommy hated me, I'd tried to win her love. If I just did everything she said, if I got good grades, if I did all my chores, if I behaved and kept my room clean, then I might make her proud and earn her love.

By the time I was eight, I knew better, but until then the agony of her punishments wrapped me in a cocoon of constant suffering. I blamed myself for failing. I wasn't good enough. I had to be better.

"How about we have lunch tomorrow, and after that, we'll see," I suggested.

She nodded, still looking like a kicked puppy. "Of course. Where would you like to meet?"

"How about The Yard? It's got a couple dozen really good food trucks and great seating." Not to mention a bar. We might both need drinks to get through this.

"Sure. That sounds delightful."

I was pretty sure that compared to blue fin tuna and white truffles, it sounded like dog vomit, but I appreciated her attempt at enthusiasm. Hopefully she'd be pleasantly surprised by the offerings.

"Meet there at noon?" I asked.

"I'll be there."

We awkwardly stood there a moment. "Well, I'm on my way to meet someone. I'd better go, or I'll be late."

"Of course. I didn't mean to keep you." She hesitated like she wanted to say more but then turned away and headed for her Porsche.

I waved as she drove out, glancing down at Ajax, who'd flopped down in my shadow, panting happily. "That was excruciating. I need fortification before this meeting. Let's get some ice cream."

He followed me to the car and hopped across my seat into the passenger seat.

"I swear you have springs in your butt. That, or you levitate."

I slid into my seat and rubbed his ears. As always, he rolled onto his back presenting me with his agonizingly itchy tummy. I obeyed his silent command, chuckling as he squirmed and moaned with delight. After a couple minutes, I started the car and drove out, still scratching him with my free hand.

I opted for two scoops, one of caramel macchiato, the other of chocolate espresso. I also drove through a coffee place and picked up a high octane mocha and a puppuccino for Ajax.

"You can't have any licks of ice cream," I told him firmly. "It isn't good for you, so you can just stop with the dying-of-hunger eyes. Remember I *know* what you've eaten today. I'm not buying the *woe is me act.*"

He made a sad sound and curled up on the seat, muzzle propped on his front paws as he continued to cast forlorn looks at me.

I shook my head and held the cone out for him. He swiped his tongue across the ice cream a couple of times before I withdrew the offering.

"No more. I may be a softie but not so much that I'll let you get sick on my watch. I want to keep you around for as long as possible."

He gave a hefty sigh and wriggled around so that he could lay his head on my thigh. His eyes drifted shut.

I couldn't help my smile as I sped down the road. I might not know if I was in love with Damon, but I was head-over-heels for Ajax. My furry boyfriend.

# CHAPTER THREE

I had to drive out past my inherited estate to get to my appointment. I was headed to a little town about ten miles east of Sweetwater. I drove along the river for a short while, and then up into the hills, dotted here and again with groves of oaks and tinted blue-green with bursts of yellow from the invading star-thistle. Flame-colored poppies grew along the fence lines, burning like fire against the dried, gold grass.

I rolled my windows down to allow the warm summery scents to wrap around me. Ajax sat up and propped his front feet on the window sill to sniff the air, his thick hair ruffling in the wind.

It wasn't long before I topped a hill and began the descent into Sutton. It was a picturesque little town of about fifteen thousand people, nestled in a lush green valley. They grew grapes here and a number of other crops. The town itself was quirky and quite a tourist destination. It claimed to be centered on the intersection of two ley lines, with a vortex circling around the entire town. A lot of shops were therefore devoted to new-agey sorts of things, crystals and herbs, Native American artwork and jewelry, candles, perfumes, oils, bookstores, yarn shops, herb and tea shops, craft shops, and so on, plus the usual wine shops, bakeries, cafes, bistros, and not to mention a haunted luxury hotel and spa.

The latter sat in the middle of the town on the opposite side of the central green from the courthouse. The Hotel Varonne had been built in the gold rush by an eccentric family from France of the same name. The spa had been added when hot springs were discovered just before World War I. Walnut trees and oaks surrounded the spacious grounds, and a meditation labyrinth wound through a flower and herb garden.

The downtown spiraled out from the green, the narrow streets curving and twisting like Medusa's hair. It wasn't the most efficient design, nor all that easy to navigate, and generally whenever I visited, I parked outside the down-town maze and walked.

Today I pulled into the lot between the old-fashioned ice-cream parlor and Fuller's Pharmacy and General Store. I got out and stretched. Ajax hopped down beside me and shook out his fur. As warm as it was, I couldn't leave him in the car, even with all the windows down.

I checked the address for the store where I was meeting my potential client and swung into a swift walk. I had twenty minutes until the meeting and would be there in ten. I stopped for a couple bottles of water from a sidewalk coffee kiosk. I had a collapsible bowl for Ajax in my purse.

The town was gearing up for its annual Renaissance Faire, which would be held on the green and spill over onto the Hotel Varonne's grounds as well as into the streets. Many of those nearest the green would be closed to allow people to walk in the roads and for street performers to do their thing.

The Faire lasted nearly four weeks, and people came from all over to attend. Jen, Stacey, Lorraine, and I looked forward to it every year. The entertainment included plays, music, dancers, magicians, jousting, and raptor demonstrations, among many other things. The food was always delicious, as was the beer and wine.

The decorations had already begun to go up, including tinkling bells and chimes that hung everywhere and created fairytale music. I had a hard time not stopping to look in the store windows to see the artful displays that seemed to grow more grand and detailed every year. It didn't hurt that there was a contest for the best one, the funniest, the most unusual, and so on.

I hurried my steps when I realized I'd dawdled a little too long, and I was about to be late. A three-story building, Mitzi's Emporium was wedged between a tea shop and an antique store. Its name scrolled across the windows in gold letters. Underneath in smaller lettering read: Where You Will Always Find the Answers You Seek. I wondered what kinds of answers Mitzi's sold. Peeking through the dim and dusty windows, I could see racks of clothing and displays full of all sorts of tchotchkes. An eclectic mix of things for sure.

I dug out Ajax's bowl and filled it with water. "Stay out here. I'll be back soon," I told him. I knocked on the wood door frame and then tried to open the doors. They were locked. I checked the time again. I was exactly on time. I knocked again, louder.

"Oh, hello," came a woman's voice behind me. "You must be Beck Wyatt. We're around in the courtyard. It's such a lovely afternoon, we thought we'd have lemonade while we discuss the estate."

I turned around. The speaker was a diminutive woman, maybe five foot three, with narrow features, straight brown hair caught up in a clip behind her head, purple cat eye glasses, and wearing jeans and a tank top beneath an over-sized plaid flannel shirt, its sleeves rolled up above her elbows. She appeared to be my age, perhaps a little older.

"I'm Beck," I said. "You must be Lindsey?" I held out my hand.

"I am." She held up her hands, both encased in tight-fitting gloves. "I'm sorry, I don't shake hands. I have arthritis and wear compression gloves. Shaking hands can be very painful."

"That can't be fun."

"It isn't. Won't you follow me? My cousins, Rhi and Lorel, are waiting for us."

I followed her along a little cobblestone walkway that passed through a green tunnel made of trellised vines and emptied into a round cobbled patio behind the building. A dry fountain sat in the center with a dozen planters full of both overgrown and dying plants. A shady table sat under a mountain ash. It held a pitcher of lemonade and a plate of cookies and fruit. Two women rose as we arrived.

They were clearly identical twins, though one had her pale blonde locks cut in a layered pixie and the other wore her silky hair long. They both towered over their cousin, standing about my height, which was five foot eight. Both looked vaguely ethereal with their pale skin, long fingers, and delicate figures. They wore gorgeous summery dresses that looked like they cost a fortune. "These are my cousins Rhiannon and Lorelei," Lindsey said. Her gestures indicated that the short-haired one was Rhiannon and the long-haired one was Lorelei. "My aunt was a fan of seventies rock music and took their names from songs."

Both women smiled brightly. "So good to meet you," Rhiannon said. "Call me Rhi. Please sit down. Is that your dog?"

I glanced behind me to see that Ajax had followed us and now lay where the cobblestone walk met the patio.

"That's Ajax," I confirmed. "He's friendly."

"May we pet him?" asked Lorelei.

"Come here, Ajax," I told him, patting my leg. He sprang up and trotted over, his tongue flopping out of his mouth. He politely sat beside me as the two women introduced themselves and pet him.

"Does he need anything? Water maybe?" Lindsey stood a couple feet away, watching her cousins fawn over Ajax, who was reveling in the attention.

"I gave him some water out front. I left the bowl—"

She didn't wait for me to finish but gave a sharp little nod. "No problem. I'll get it. Have a seat."

She trotted off. I sat down at an empty seat. Rhi and Lorelei sat on either side of me.

"Do help yourself," Lorelei said, nudging a clean plate toward me. "Can I pour you lemonade? It's fresh squeezed with a little bit of mint."

"Please," I said and put a couple of cookies and some blueberries on my plate.

Lindsey returned and put Ajax's bowl down in the shade near me, took her seat opposite me, and immediately got down to business.

"My aunt Mitzi died a little while ago. I'm the executor of her will. I can show you those papers and her death certificate, as I'm sure you'll need to see them to be assured we are authorized to liquidate the place. She left everything to Rhi and Lorel, who want to sell the contents of both the shop and the living space above. We'd like to get a bid from you and see when we could schedule a sale."

I nodded. "I'll have to walk through and see what's here and if it's a sale we can do. We generally charge fifty percent of the proceeds, which includes advertisement, staffing, preparation, the sale itself, and cleanup. That percentage may be adjusted upward depending on the condition of the estate pieces and how much cleaning and organizing will be necessary. You'll also need to rent a dumpster for anything that's broken, moldy, moth-eaten, or otherwise unsalable. Some items of greater value I may take and sell at auction or to dealers if I think we can get a higher price that way. Keep in mind the estates I take on are higher end with more valuable art, collectibles, and furniture."

Lindsey nodded, having heard pretty much the same spiel when she'd first contacted me.

"Have you removed or tagged the things that you wish to keep?" I asked.

"We're not keeping anything," Lindsey said adamantly.

"That's unusual. Not even family heirlooms or mementos?"

"The will specifically forbids me from taking anything," Lindsey said. "My aunt did not like me. The feeling was more than mutual."

"And she made you her executor?"

"It was her last slap at Lindsey," said Lorelei—or Lorel, as Lindsey called her. "Our mother was vindictive and mean and making Lindsey the executor was her way of rubbing Lindsey's nose in the fact that she was getting nothing, and we were getting everything."

Rhi reached out and put a hand on her cousin's forearm and gave it a little squeeze. "She knew that Lindsey wouldn't refuse. She's always been there for us, no matter how awful Mom was."

"Which is why," Lorel said, looking at Lindsey, "we'll be giving you half of everything."

Lindsey shook her head. "The will specifically states I get nothing."

Rhi snorted. "Once we inherit, she can't tell us what to do. If we want to share our good fortune with you, then we will."

"You are sweet, but it's unnecessary. Anyhow, the will has stipulations against that."

"Our mom stole your mom's half of the shop and left you and her with nothing. She wouldn't even help when Aunt Lace needed treatment. She let her own sister die because of some feud that didn't even matter. We're just giving back what's rightfully yours, and we won't take no for an answer. We'll fight it in court if we have to."

I listened to the exchange, fascinated. Clearly the three cousins had grown up close, despite the twins' mother being a toxic bitch. Or that's what I took from the conversation. Lindsey's eyes had misted, and she gave a watery smile to her cousins, too choked up to speak.

Right about then I decided that I'd be taking the sale on, no matter what the stuff inside looked like. Aunt Mitzi sounded a little too much like Aunty Mommy for my taste, and these women deserve better.

"I'm sorry," Lindsey said to me, cheeks flushed as she crumbled a cookie on her plate. "You don't need to hear us airing dirty laundry. Aunt Mitzi wasn't so bad. She took me in after my mother died."

"Because she could turn you into Cinderella and berate you constantly, while making you do all her scut work," Rhi said. "Don't go painting her into a saint. When Aunt Lace died and Mom couldn't hurt her any more, she decided she'd go after you. She didn't take you in out of the goodness of her heart; she did it to make it easier to mess with you."

"She sounds like a winner," I said.

"She was anything but," Lorel said. "Much as we wanted to love her and even did, we could see what she was. None of us want to keep anything that reminds us of her. So every last little scrap has to go."

"After that, we'll get an exorcist in here and make sure she's gone before we open up our own store," Rhi declared.

"Rhi!" Lindsey admonished. "Don't say things like that. Miss Wyatt will think we're crazy."

"Why not say it?" the other woman argued. "Mom always said she'd haunt the place. You know as well as I do that if she could stay and make our lives miserable, she would. An exorcism is the only way we can be sure."

"And if that doesn't work, we'll nuke it from space," Lorel added darkly. "It's the only way to be sure."

I laughed at that. "First, everybody please call me Beck. Second, I'd totally do the same." In fact, I was thinking I should have already done some sort of cleanse on the estate to make sure Aunty Mommy really had toddled off to hell when she died. "Now, are you ready to show me around?"

"Sure," Lindsey said, standing. She hesitated. "You should probably know that this place really is a little weird. I'm not saying that Aunt Mitzi is haunting the place, but—" She shrugged.

Curiouser and curiouser. Did that mean someone else was haunting it? There were strange sounds and unaccountable cold spots? What kind of weird were they talking about? I wanted to ask, but figured they wouldn't tell me the truth at the risk of sounding like lunatics. Anyhow, I'd find out soon enough.

I stood as the twins did. "The town is famous for its mystical heritage. It would be strange if there *wasn't* something odd in most places here, right?" I said brightly.

Lindsey's smile was slightly strained. "We've definitely got *odd* covered. Come on. I'll show you."

"Don't worry," Lorel said as she took my arm. Rhi took the other. "We'll make sure you're safe."

I smiled. Magic pulsed in my blood. Little did they know that I was probably far more strange than whatever was going on in the building. I pushed my shield out to encompass Ajax, who padded along at my heels. Whatever might happen inside, I wasn't about to risk him, even if all we were facing down were mutant dust-bunnies.

# CHAPTER FOUR

We entered through the back of the shop. Dusty shades covered the windows. Thin carpet covered the floor. Lindsey flipped a switch, and a crystal chandelier cast warm light over the space. French, I'd guess. Probably from the seventeen hundreds and wired for electricity. A good omen for the rest of the merchandise.

I glanced around. I was wrong about the carpet. It was a rug. Chinese, antique, hand-knotted, and made of silk. Its colors were still vibrant, and a quick scan didn't reveal any stains or damage. Glass cabinets jammed with all sorts of things crowded together along the walls. In the center stood a glass-topped oak pedestal table. The pedestal column was shaped like a tree, its limbs stretching to hold up the glass table top. At the bottom, carved roots spread out in a circle to create the base. Four matching chairs with purple silk seats completed the set.

A black silk square sat centered on the top. Different colored candles in silver holders anchored the cloth in place, along with a polished silver bowl on a wood base.

Heavy brass floor candelabras created a square around the table.

I scanned the walls and then the ceiling. Symbols and numbers covered every open space. A few constellations, some runes, Egyptian hieroglyphics, and a bunch of stuff I didn't recognize.

What startled me was the magic permeating the room. I could feel it like a low hum vibrating through my body. I glanced at my companions. They looked at me as if waiting for my reaction. To the magic? Or the whole mystical vibe? I didn't know if I should say anything or not.

"I take it this is where your aunt answered customer questions," I said, settling on a middle ground. "Like it says on the front door sign. Did she read palms? Tarot? Tea leaves? Perform seances?" I kept my voice neutral.

"All of it," Lorel said. She didn't look embarrassed, which meant, what? Mitzi had been a witch? Or just that she'd accepted her mother's eccentricities?

"Was she any good at it?"

That question seemed to surprise both Lorel and Rhi.

"Somebody was always coming in for readings," Rhi said. "She had to take on extra help because she got so busy with it." There was a shifty quality to the way she looked away. She was lying about something.

"She had a lot of clients, according to her books, but I live in the Sacramento area and didn't visit often," Lindsey added.

"It's very theatrical," I said. I disentangled myself from the twins and toured the room. The curio cabinets contained an enormous variety of things, some that I knew were valuable, others that weren't, and a whole lot that I'd have to research. "The furniture is high quality. Those, the rug, and chandelier will net a decent profit for you. I can get more specific when I inventory the cabinets."

"The store room is through there," Lindsey said, pulling back a gauzy wall hanging to reveal a door painted to look like the walls and ceiling. "It's small. She kept most of her merchandise on the floor. A lot of it is one of a kind anyway. Most of what's in there arrived after she died, or she hadn't had a chance to put it on display." She moved to another entry, this one covered by heavy swaths of velvet cloth. "This takes us to the store."

The opening actually led to a small kitchenette with a bathroom for employees only. From there, we stepped out into the retail space. Rhi and Lorel scooted close to me while Lindsey turned on the rest of the lights.

To say the space was eclectic would have been like calling Disneyland a school playground. The colors made me feel like I'd walked into a kaleidoscope. Or maybe I was on an acid trip.

There had to be at least a dozen chandeliers hanging from a midnight blue ceiling painted to look like a night sky. Between them, crystals hung everywhere, splashing rainbows all around and adding to the color chaos. The aisles were like rabbit trails: narrow and winding with no particular pattern.

The rear of the shop contained a little clothing boutique and a small dressing room. The clothes were stunning, and no two were the same.

"These are lovely," I said, examining a dress. "Well-made."

"I designed that one," Lorel said.

I lifted my brows. "You're a clothing designer? It's gorgeous. Did you create the dress you're wearing, too?"

She looked down at herself. "No, Rhi made this one."

"You both design?"

Lorel nodded. "We want to convert the entire store to focus on our clothes."

"Alright, then. Show me around."

The rest of the store contained an unusual mix of items to say the least, all set out in random order, as far as I could tell. I saw clay sculptures, blown glass, metal art, paintings, drawings, textiles, and more. One little corner nook held prayer rugs and pashminas. Another had snow globes, polished rocks and minerals, crystal balls, god and goddess statuettes, and various religious paraphernalia, most of it pagan related. Jewelry cases surrounded the cash register in the middle of the room. A knife and sword display filled a little cul-de-sac near the front.

A discreet corner held an array of sex aids, from dildos to herbs. A tiny little sign over the small archway leading inside said: Guaranteed Orgasms. I blinked. Guaranteed? And if the customer didn't have one, had Aunt Mitzi taken it back and returned the money? And then what? Resold it?

I shuddered. Not a particularly appetizing thought.

"Upstairs in the loft are lotions and other bath products, yarn, and um, I guess you'd call them witchy remedies," Lindsey said. "Aromatherapy, oils, tinctures, and that sort of thing. They're all labeled as some kind of witch's brew, though. I guess to fit the town's mystique. There's also a lot of books on witchcraft, herbals, alchemy, and so on. Those have been popular and turn over relatively quickly."

"I'd like to have a look."

We went up the iron stairs and the loft space was no less packed.

One thing was clear, however. The general craftsmanship of the inventory was high. I recognized the names of several local and not so local artists. Cataloging and prepping the store for a sale was going to take some time, however.

I looked at Lorel and Rhi. "Are you two absolutely sure you don't want to keep anything? Because once we have a contract, it all gets sold."

The three other women exchanged a look.

"We can't keep anything," Rhi said, not quite meeting my gaze.

"*We* don't want to," Lorel corrected. "Lindsey *can't*."

"So everything inside the building goes up for sale, including your aunt's personal belongings? All the fixtures, racks, shelves, display cases, and so on? What about your clothing?"

All three nodded, but I could tell they didn't want to say yes, and I could also tell that they had no intention of enlightening me about the situation. So, of course I decided to push.

"Didn't you say you wanted to open your own store? Wouldn't you want to keep some basics to facilitate the new business? Like racks and shelves? And why give up your designs? You won't get a fraction of the price you should."

"Rhi and Lorel plan to renovate and put their own stamp on the place," Lindsey said. "Start with an entire new look, and this stuff just doesn't fit the vision."

"Rhi, Lorel, *and Lindsey* you mean," Rhi told her cousin. "This place is going to belong to all three of us." She looked at me. "Lindsey designs stunning jewelry and accessories. The will stipulates she can't take anything whatsoever from Mitzi's estate, so we want to sell it all."

"Don't those stipulations include the property itself?"

"We've got a plan to get around that, but it will be easier if we follow the letter of the will."

"Still, dumping such pretty designs for pennies on the dollar is harsh."

Rhi grimaced. "These aren't our favorite designs anyhow; our mother always had an opinion, and we had to modify accordingly."

Lorel gave a humorless smile. "Or else."

I wondered what that meant, but before I could ask, Lindsey broke in.

"There's some really beautiful amethyst and citrine cathedrals next to the sword display," she said, clearly uncomfortable with the direction the conversation had taken. "Why don't you go back downstairs to look? We'll just be a moment."

Translation: go away so we can talk privately.

I wandered down the stairs and found myself standing in front of a display of rings inside a round glass case on top of a tall stand. They didn't look like much. Mostly they were thin bands made from silver, gold, or copper, and set with small stones. None of them were worth more than a hundred dollars.

I rotated the case and discovered it was locked. At the same moment, Ajax growled deep in his throat and something yanked on my ponytail. I jerked and swung around, only to find myself and Ajax alone. All the hair on his back stood on end, and he continued to growl, his head swiveling in search of the enemy.

A hand in the middle of my back shoved me toward the front door. I staggered forward before catching my balance and whirling back around. Still nothing there. Cold hit me then. Icy and sharp. My breath plumed white and Ajax whined and leaned into me. A soft chortle of laughter erupted around us, sounding smug.

Oh fuck no. Not today, Aunt Mitzi. Or that's who I assumed the ghost was.

"You really want to play, bitch?" Magic curled around my fingers, but I didn't really know what to do. How does someone fight a ghost? Damon had said this morning you could bind them to an object, but how? And how did you catch them in the first place?

*You make shit up until you figure it out,* I told myself with a *duh* and a mental kick. That's the way I'd always done magic.

Damon had been teaching me actual spell-crafting, but it was like going back to kindergarten, and the basics of the traditional witching world's magic was like reading Sanskrit. Actually, it probably was Sanskrit. Or maybe if Sanskrit fucked Norse runes and had a baby that grew up and fucked calculus. The baby of *that* unholy union would be witch code. Language. Whatever.

Anyhow, I'd always just thought about what I wanted to do and made it happen. I have an obstinate streak a hundred miles wide, which means I don't know how to give up. Apparently, that's not as much a good thing as I'd like to think. Some people say I'm pigheaded, or that I have a death wish. I don't. At least, I don't walk around thinking I want to kill myself. I just don't like losing, and failing has never been an option.

I should probably see a shrink one of these days.

Something yanked my hair again. Hard. And then it bit my arm. Bit. My. Arm. It hurt like a motherfucker.

"Fuck!"

I looked down. Blood seeped through my skin wherever

the invisible teeth had gouged. Aunt Mitzi had a surprisingly big mouth.

I may have lost it. Power swelled, and I shoved it out in a blanket with the notion of flinging it around the ghost and drawing it tight like a drawstring bag with the bitey-bitch inside.

I got lucky. Or maybe it was just that Aunt Mitzi wasn't as good at ghosting as she thought.

She fought me. My magic is invisible, which is apparently abnormal, so I couldn't see her struggle, but I imagine a scene right out of Looney Toons with Bugs in a sack carried by Elmer Fudd. Or maybe Elmer in a sack carried by Bugs. Probably that.

I imagined Aunt Mitzi kicking and screaming about getting those little varmints. It felt like she was throwing a tantrum anyhow.

"What's happened? Are you all right?" Lindsey, Rhi, and Lorel had come running at my shout and now stood watching me with worried looks.

"You've got a ghost," I said, examining my arm. The bite was definitely human, and she hadn't held back. Blood had begun to trickle from where the teeth had cut through. The damned thing was going to bruise badly too. Did I need a rabies shot?

Their eyes widened as they saw the wound.

"A ghost?" Lorel echoed, trying to sound surprised, her gaze riveted on the bite.

I couldn't help rolling my eyes. Was this really the way they were going to play it? All innocence and naiveté? Not a fucking chance. I glared. "You can't be surprised. You're the ones who said the place was odd. You even hinted that your aunt was haunting the place."

"Are you okay? That looks awful. Maybe we should take you to the hospital," Rhi said, totally ignoring what I'd said.

Nope. Not going to let the subject change. "I'm fine." I grabbed a silk scarf off a nearby rack and pressed it to my wound. Aunt Mitzi was still fighting my hold, and I tightened my grip, wondering if I could squish her and if I cared if I did. "Are you going to tell me what's going on?"

And why, of all their choices, had they picked me to sell the estate? My stellar reputation? Or because I was a witch? And if the latter, how the fuck did they know that? Because it wasn't exactly public information, and all the ways I could imagine them figuring it out weren't exactly healthy for me. I wasn't exactly hiding it, but I wasn't flaunting it, either.

Rhi and Lorel looked at Lindsey, who flushed and averted her gaze. She chewed her lip. I waited, but my patience quickly thinned to fumes.

"I'm kind of psychic," she murmured finally.

"Congratulations. What does that have to do with me?"

All three of the other women stared. I guess they were expecting me to laugh at such a ridiculous assertion, or maybe they'd thought I'd freak out.

"The night Aunt Mitzi died, I started having visions. Of you. Your face. They came on strong and overwhelmed me. I'd pass out. It took me days to recover from one. Worse, I had no idea who you were. The visions grew stronger and more frequent. I couldn't sleep, and I lost track of everything."

"She went delirious sometimes," Rhi said. "We wrote down all she said, but not a lot made sense."

"It was scary," Lorel added, reaching out to grip Lindsey's hand. "We'd never seen her experience anything like it, and there wasn't anything we could do."

So much for the horrible arthritis Lindsey claimed she had. She probably just didn't want to randomly touch people and have an accidental vision, though I had no idea what I was talking about.

"How did you figure out it was me?" My tone didn't thaw, but I could hear their sincerity, which went a little way to making up for the bite.

Lindsey sighed. "I'm not a very good psychic. I've never been able to control it. It just… happens." She shook her head. "I've also never experienced visions so debilitating."

"We were afraid she was going to stroke out," Lorel said. "Rhi and I went over all her ravings. Lindsey helped when she was coherent. We finally realized she had to be talking about the shop, so we came here. We thought it would get better if we came."

"But as soon as we walked in, an ocean of images crashed over me," Lindsey said, picking up the story again. "Only this time it wasn't just images. I got sounds and smells and even taste. Everything was sharp and clear, but it all came at me so fast that my brain couldn't process it all."

"She dropped like a rock," Lorel said and tears seeped down her face. "She wouldn't wake up."

"And then the whole place started rattling. Everything danced like it was going to fly off the shelves and walls. The displays, the racks, the chandeliers—it was all rocking and spinning and thumping and the noise was so loud." Rhi shuddered, her shoulders hunching. "We dragged Lindsey out to the courtyard and then took her home. We couldn't wake her for two days. We just about took her to the hospital."

"Still doesn't explain why me," I said.

"When I woke up, I knew your name, and I knew what

you did and how to find you. I thought the visions made sense, given the shop and what we needed to do." Lindsey shrugged and went back to chewing her lip.

And I chewed on her words. I had a lot fewer questions than I would have expected from the confession. It all made sense in a fucked up way. My whole life had been fucked up, so this didn't exactly rise to the level of shocking.

"Assuming Aunt Mitzi was responsible for the whole poltergeist thing when you walked in, why did she let you come in today, or any other day for that matter?"

"We don't know," Rhi said slowly.

"But you have a guess," I said.

"Maybe she used up a lot of her power doing that and then had to recuperate. Overextended herself."

"You don't sound convinced."

Lindsey answered. "She might be planning something else. *If* it's her."

My brows rose. "You don't believe it is?" If Lindsey really was psychic, shouldn't she be able to tell?

"I'm psychic, but I don't know how to actually *do* psychic stuff. It happens to me; I don't make it happen."

"That's got to be frustrating." I allowed my sympathy to show through. I'd had to figure out my magic myself. I knew what a pain in the ass it was to bumble blindly with something that was clearly a natural part of you but came without any sort of a manual. If it *had* come with a manual, it would have been written in a language nobody had heard of and in invisible ink.

"I know things that I shouldn't. Or at least I think I know them." She tossed her hands up and strode away, then spun around and came back. "What if I'm delusional? Or what if I'm wrong? The visions don't let go unless I act, and if I don't, they practically put me in a coma." She scrubbed her hands over her face. "I'm a freak is what I am."

"You aren't delusional. If you were, you couldn't have found Beck," Lorel stoutly assured her.

"You *aren't* a freak," Rhi said. "Don't ever call yourself that again, or I swear I'll kick your ass."

Lindsey gave her a 'get real' look.

"I'll do it," Rhi insisted. "Even if I have to get help. Lorelei will help, won't you?"

"I'd hate to but of course. Can't have Lindsey running around bullying herself. Bullying is wrong."

I couldn't help cracking a smile. Neither could Lindsey, which I suspected was the point.

"It doesn't really matter who's haunting the place. The fact is, you've got a ghost."

All three looked over their shoulders uneasily. I didn't tell them I'd captured her. I wasn't ready to reveal I was a witch.

"That's why we have to sell everything. Once it's all gone, we can do a cleansing with a shaman or something, and she'll have to leave," Rhi said.

I had doubts about that. "So you don't expect *me* to get rid of Aunt Mitzi?"

Lindsey shook her head. "You arrange estate sales. That must be why the visions pushed me to find you. Anyway, you couldn't get rid of my aunt." She hesitated. "Could you?"

"Not that I know of." I could have told her that her visions had brought her to me for more than my professional expertise. It was too much a coincidence that I was a witch, and these women had a supernatural infestation. It didn't make me a liar, though. I didn't know if I could exorcize Aunt Mitzi. Damon might know how.

I remembered he was on a flight to who knew where at the moment. Could he get texts on a plane? Probably, but did I want to bother him? He might freak out that I was about to do something dangerous.

With my Uncle Mason on his own trip somewhere, that left asking my mom, which was a whole other kettle of rotting fish. I tabled the question.

All three women looked unnerved, disappointed, and resigned. Meanwhile, Aunt Mitzi had gone into super spasms, and I wasn't sure how long I could keep holding her. The magical sack I'd put her in had begun to fray, and I was playing a game of plug the dike. Sooner or later she'd break free, unless I figured out a better container. Where were the ghostbusters when I needed them?

Getting drunk, probably. I was certainly beginning to think it was a fantastic idea.

"I guess you don't want to do the sale, then?" Lindsey asked.

And leave Aunt Mitzi to terrorize these three forever? Oh hell no. "I'll do it."

All three gaped.

"Why?" asked Rhi.

"Because *I* happen to know why the visions brought you to me. I'm a witch."

All three recoiled.

"You don't need to make fun of us because we believe in psychics," Lorel snapped. "Lindsey has a gift. A *real* gift."

"I know," I said, but my words were drowned out by Rhi's indignation. She planted her hands on her hips, jaw jutting.

"Do you have any idea how hard Lindsey's had it? She's been bullied most her life because of her gift. People like you ridicule her and tease her and call her all sorts of names, and when they find out she really is psychic, they avoid her or spread rumors. It's a modern version of a mob with pitchforks and torches coming to drive her out of town. She's been fired from I don't know how many jobs for being weird or creepy or whatever. And now you're making fun of her, too. You can go straight to hell and your big-ass dog too!"

Lindsey didn't speak, her face pale and set. She blinked, clearly trying not to cry.

"All right. Suit yourselves," I said. I wasn't mad, but I also wasn't feeling particularly charitable. How could someone believe in psychics and not be at least open to the possibility that other magical creatures existed? They'd jumped to conclusions about me, just like they thought I had about Lindsey.

I could have explained myself, but I had minimal patience on a good day. Only a handful of people knew I was a witch, and I was fine keeping it that way. I'd only said something to these women because Aunt Mitzi sounded about as evil and demented as Aunty Mommy, and I could empathize. My empathy had limits, however.

"Cover your asses. I've been keeping your ghost under wraps, and she's pissed as hell. She'll probably throw a tantrum when I let her go. Good luck and have a nice day."

I let go of my magic as I headed for the door, Ajax trotting at my heels. I figured I had about five to twenty seconds before she broke free and went on a rampage. I didn't dawdle. I've seen enough ghost movies to want to be clear of the epicenter when she went nova.

We made it to the front door right when she escaped. The store turned frigid and ice crawled up the walls and frosted the windows. The pressure in the shop dropped, and my ears popped. Power laced with rage thundered against me like breaking waves. I pushed on the door, but it was still locked.

All around the store, tchotchkes, clothing, art, jewelry, swords and everything else began rising up in the air, revolving in a slow circle. Call it Geriatric Hurricane Mitzi. I had a feeling that slow spin would soon accelerate to buzz saw speeds, and when it did, anything left in the store was going to be sushi.

I sent a zap of magic into the lock. It clicked and I thrust the door open. It shoved me back and slammed shut. Fucking Mitzi.

"What's happening?" Lorel shouted over the angry buzzing that had swelled from a low hum to a loud grinding. Like a bunch of stone giants gnashing their teeth.

The three women huddled close as more and more things floated up to join the slow-motion tornado. It wheeled around them and as I expected, started picking up speed. Glass shattered as items crashed through the display cases, escaping into the whirl. The razor-edged glass followed along with everything else that wasn't nailed down. Oddly, the chandeliers didn't even sway.

Mitzi the bitchy ghost had more control than I'd hoped.

Ice glazed the windows and hardened. More ran up over the door, making it even harder to escape. I turned back to the terrified women and cast a shield around them. I'd only learned how to make them recently and wasn't sure how long it would hold. Long enough, I hoped.

Then things got worse, because of course they did. The scabbards on the swords slid off and the weapons started twirling like parade batons. It appeared Mitzi wasn't going to be satisfied with merely killing us, she wanted to mulch us, too. Already the swords had started shredding whatever came within reach.

I thought I could blow a hole in the side of the building to get us out, but she could easily follow. I needed to shut her down. Fast. The spinning had begun to speed up. I could feel pressure tugging me and my hair lifted and invisible wind plucked at my clothes. Ajax growled.

"It's okay," I told him, my mind racing.

Witches use a lot of various spells that include metals, paper, plants—you name it and some witch has probably used it—but in the end, it all boils down to the caster's intent, determination, focus, and tolerance for pain. Okay, the last isn't necessarily true, but pain happened often enough that I'd decided it was one of the four foundation stones of magic.

I did all of my magic without spells because I'd never learned how to make them. I was pretty good at it, too, since I had determination—some might say stubbornness—in spades, relentless focus (ask me how to hold a grudge), and an ability to stay focused through intense pain, thanks to Aunty Mommy. Intent was the hardest part. Aka, figuring out what the hell to do.

I didn't have time to consider, so I went the triage route. First, eliminate the immediate threat. That meant safely grounding the flying debris first, then dealing with Mitzi. I had a feeling the first would be a lot easier than the second. Especially since I had no idea how to exorcize a ghost. Or kill one. *Could* a ghost be killed? They were already dead, weren't they?

I snorted at myself. Here I was congratulating myself on my focus and then letting my mind wander. Sometimes I wondered if I was too stupid to live.

Easy money to bet Mitzi would attack as soon as I put a stop to her carousel of death and dismemberment. So that meant I really needed to deal with her at the same time. I'd caught her last time because I had a sense of where she was, but this time it wouldn't be so easy.

I scowled as I considered the options, then shook my head. I didn't have time to ponder solutions. The tornado had accelerated and the sound had grown to a roar. We were almost out of time.

The air pulled inward, dragging me a step forward. I cemented myself to the floor, and then flung a wad of sticky magic into the air. I told it to split up into as many strands as needed to grab all the stuff whirling in the air. And I told it not to tangle up as it whirled. Good thing magic didn't have to make scientific sense, or the physics would never work for this. Or maybe it was supposed to and I just didn't give a fuck about physics, and so my intent overrode the natural order. It was my backup plan, anyhow, in case things went to hell before I could snare myself a ghost.

With half my mind concentrating on grabbing up the flying objects, I released power in a flat wave until it reached wall to wall. I poured more in, running it up the walls and then ceiling, so that it enclosed the entire space. I started shrinking it, which was made more difficult by maintaining my other project. I was really hoping to get myself and the three women clear before Mitzi started her rampage.

It belatedly occurred to me that I could drop the first spell and focus on collapsing the second as fast as possible instead of splitting my focus, since the second would contain Mitzie and her ammunition. In the exact moment that I dropped it, Mitzi deployed her tornado, pushing it down and out to encompass the entire space. Things whizzed past and bounced off my protective shield. I might have heard screams from Lindsey, Rhi, and Lorel but couldn't be sure with the noise from Mitzi's would-be-fatal tantrum. I knew their shield remained, so they were safe enough for the moment.

I drew hard on my magic bubble, careful to maintain its strength as I shrank its size. Damon had made me all too aware that you had to consider each piece of the spell so you didn't end up with giant holes in it, or worse, giant holes in yourself. The result of his teaching me this had been me seriously over-thinking, instead of relying on myself like I had always done. He told me I'd been lucky. I told him I was just good. He'd rocked my confidence though, and I was doubting myself.

The roaring sound dimmed as the whirlwind stopped moving and everything crammed together. Mitzi wasn't happy. She shrieked. A demonic sound that sent prickles of ice down my spine. She fought hard, and I wound my magic around the entire mess, deciding overkill was the better part of glory, not to mention survival.

I contemplated the hovering mess, trying to decide what to do next. I needed to extract Mitzi and then set all the rest of the crap on the floor, though I doubted enough survived for a decent sale. Apparently, Mitzi didn't like her daughters consorting with their enemy cousin and plan-ning to make Lindsey part-owner of the new business.

A shiver ran through me, and a droplet of cold water landed on my forehead. I looked up to the ceiling. Melting icicles hung like stalactites from the chandeliers.

Abruptly the shrieking cut off. My stomach curled. That couldn't be good.

"What's happening?" Rhi asked in a shaky voice.

I flicked a glance at her. She had gone a pale shade of gray and stared wide-eyed at the hovering mass of crap. A cloud of junk. Made me think of the garbage patch in the ocean.

"I don't know," Lorel replied softly.

"It's got to be Aunt Mitzi. What's she trying to do?" Lindsey, this time.

"She's trying to kill you and still would be if I let her," I said a little more acerbically than I intended. Bet they believed I was a witch now. I resisted the urge to say *I told you so*. Barely. Instead, I said, "You're welcome and shut up. This is only a temporary fix. I need to figure out how to send her to hell where she clearly belongs."

I didn't bother checking their reactions. I didn't have the bandwidth for them. Mitzi had begun pulverizing everything inside my trap. It didn't do her any good. The more she made confetti, the more my bubble condensed, making her trap smaller. Unless that was the point. Maybe she wanted it smaller? I couldn't see any reason why, but then I wasn't a poltergeist with control issues and an anger management problem.

"Mitzi! What exactly is your problem? You're dead. You've been voted off the island. Time to go, or I'll have to make you go."

She shrieked again, louder, and it actually hurt my ears and made my eyeballs vibrate in my head.

"Well I would let you go, but you're a menace, not to mention batshit crazy. I mean, you were trying to murder your own daughters, not to mention your niece, who, I might add, is trying to follow your will to its last shitty letter. You ought to be grateful to her, instead of throwing a murder tantrum."

As I spoke, an idea began to gel, but I didn't have a handle on how to get it done.

Then Mitzi went quiet. Too quiet.

"So you're ghosting us now," I said. "Irony

notwithstanding, we appreciate the quiet and feel free to leave."

She didn't respond. Lindsey let out a low moan and crumpled to her knees, holding her head. She tipped sideways and curled into the fetal position.

"What's wrong?" I asked.

Both Rhi and Lorel had dropped to their knees beside their cousin but refrained from touching her.

"She's having a vision," Rhi said when I repeated my question. She sounded worried.

"Is she going to be alright?"

"Yes."

I couldn't tell if that was certainty or wishful thinking. I decided I couldn't worry about her and Mitzi at the same time, and Mitzi required my attention.

What I wanted to do was send her off to wherever she belonged, but I didn't know where that was, and I probably couldn't do it anyhow. That left containing her as best I could. I decided to go with binding her to some object. If I could limit how far she could wander or affect the world around her, that would be enough. Then I could stick her in a safety deposit box or maybe throw her in the ocean.

I sighed, remembering that magic didn't hold up to the elements, and I was pretty sure that ocean water would be fastest at eroding it. Not a chance I was willing to take.

I looked around for something I could use. Metal would probably be best. More durable than any of my other choices, unless I could find a rock. My eye caught on the tall amethyst cathedrals that Mitzi hadn't bothered with. Beside them were shelves that had held rocks and minerals. My gaze slid to a spear of pink quartz that had fallen on the floor and broke in two. One piece was about an inch by two inches, with one rough end and one pointed end.

Ghosts had no mass, so size shouldn't matter. I picked up the smaller chunk of quartz and rubbed my fingers over it, thinking.

Lindsey started talking, but I couldn't understand what she was saying. I blocked her out and concentrated on solving my Mitzi problem.

Once again, I realized I was overthinking, and I needed to do what I did best. Decide what to do and do it. I had to have full confidence in my abilities. Damon would call it cockiness. He'd warn me not to be rash, that I had to pay attention to potential consequences and hedge against them.

I drew a breath and let it out. Fuck all that. I knew my magic, and I knew how to use it. Sure, it wasn't conventional, but it worked for me.

"I can do this," I muttered, though whether to reassure myself or the absent Damon. "I'm damned well *going* to do this."

With that, I went to work. Mitzi had been caught inside my bubble. Now I just needed to extract her and bind her to the quartz. I formed a new bubble just inside the old one. This one was to allow anything to pass through it except Mitzi. Sticky anemone-style arms covered the interior, helping to immobilize her once she was caught.

I contracted the interior bubble. It passed easily over the debris, reducing it down to a tiny ball of energy, no larger than a marble. I pulled it down to land in my empty palm. My magic was invisible, but Mitzi was a swirling drop of black, blue, and yellow. The colors twisted around themselves but didn't mix.

I set the chunk of quartz on top of her in my hand. Made of nothing but energy, she passed easily inside. Now I had to make it permanent. Deciding to take no chances, I created a needle and thread and stitched her inside, stabbing her over and over and wrapping the binding thread around the stone. I took my time. I made sure she'd be able to see and hear everything around her, but she wouldn't be able to use her poltergeist powers, leaving her helpless.

When I decided she wasn't going anywhere, I wrapped my hand around the stone and sealed the bindings inside. I opened my hand and lifted it up to the level of my eyes.

"Welcome home, Mitzi," I said. "I don't know what made you so bitter or mean, but you're not going to hurt your daughters or niece anymore. If, by some insane chance, you should decide you want to be a helpful ghost, one who guards and protects, I'll know, and I might just set you free. But I don't plan to hold my breath. Few people recover from being assholes, though would taking a day or two off have killed you?"

I tossed her into the air and she fastened onto one of the chandeliers where she'd have a good seat to see all that happened in the place. Next I lowered the hovering mass of stuff to the floor and left it in a pile in the middle of the room.

Lindsey still lay on the floor. She writhed and her mouth opened and closed in gasps, her face twisting in pain. She no longer made any coherent sounds. Her eyes had rolled back up into her head, so now they looked eerily white, like a zombie.

I wandered over. "She going to be all right?"

Lorel looked up at me. "This one's bad. I'm not sure her body can take it."

"Can I help?"

Rhi shook her head. "Nobody can."

I looked around at the destruction around us. "Should

you move her somewhere more comfortable? How long is she likely to be like this?"

Lindsey herself answered. Her body snapped stiff and straight, her fingers curling into claws. She closed her eyes and her face relaxed. When she lifted her eyelids again, her eyes had rolled back down and appeared normal. She blinked and looked around. Her gaze settled on me.

"Be careful. Something bad is going to happen. It's coming for you."

She passed out.

# CHAPTER FIVE

I found myself on the road an hour later and wondering just what kind of trouble was on its way. Lindsey had said it was bad, but that pretty much defined most of my life up until this point. She probably thought the Mitzi situation was bad. I'd come away unscathed, so I considered it an easy day. Of course I didn't know when or if they'd ever be able to have an estate sale with the damage done to all of their inventory, but I told them to call me when they sorted things out.

I'd also told them where they could find Aunt Mitzi, and they'd decided to leave her hanging from the chandelier for the time being. Lorel and Rhi had both apologized for doubting that I was a witch, and both had thanked me profusely for disarming their mother and trapping her. Says a lot when your own kids want you locked up. Lindsey hadn't said much of anything after her proclamation that something was coming for me. She'd pretty much gone catatonic.

Her cousins had helped her outside into a chaise lounge, where they forced her to drink some lemonade before she fell asleep. The cousins predicted she would remain sleeping for at least twenty-four hours, if not several days, waking only to eat, drink, and use the toilet. Not that she'd truly be awake, Lorel explained. Just that her body would recognize its needs and prompt her to care for herself. Her brain would remain off-line, however, until it recovered. Or at least that was their experience.

I set aside all thoughts of the three women and turned my attention to bad possibilities. I really had no idea what could possibly happen. I didn't like imagining bad things, as I didn't want to invite trouble, and I had a feeling that my imagination was worse than reality could muster. I didn't actually care if something happened to me, but the idea of something happening to Stacey, Jen, Lorraine, or Damon, made my stomach knot.

By the time I got back to town, I'd decided not to worry about it. It wasn't productive. I could worry when it happened. Maybe I'd even put it on my calendar.

It was after seven when I returned to Damon's hotel room, after having run a couple errands. I fed Ajax before I showered and changed into black jeans, black boots, black T-shirt, and a black bra and underwear just to be consistent. Not that anybody was going to see me naked or even almost naked. Of course I said that several times before, only to be proven wrong. It never hurts to be prepared.

I cleaned the bite Mitzi had given me and covered it with a large Band-Aid. It had started to bruise. Did I need rabies shots?

I texted the girls to make sure we were still on for the evening. Lorraine's reply said she couldn't make it, since she had an emergency coming in and expected the surgery to last well into the morning. Apparently, there'd been a collision between a pickup pulling a horse trailer and an RV.

Mostly Lorraine dealt with small animals, but several horses had been injured, and there were only two large animal vets in the area. Those were taking the more critical horses, but it was clear the animal Lorraine would be operating on was in nearly as bad condition.

I asked her if she wanted me to be there, but she said no. I'm something of an animal whisperer. For some reason they trust me, even when they're out of their skulls with terror, or in a frenzied rage. I'd never actually worked with horses, but I'd never met an animal I couldn't calm. Lorraine said she might need me once the horse woke up from its anesthesia, but until then I couldn't be useful.

I texted Jen and Stacey to let them know and made arrangements to have dinner with Jen and afterward meet Stacey at the club where she worked as a bartender. We were on a mission tonight. One of the waitresses at The Starlight Club had an ex who had a problem letting go and had been giving her all sorts of hell. More than once he'd taken her car and abandoned it somewhere, forcing her to pay towing fees and once pay to get it out of the police impound lot. He'd called the cops on her more than once, reporting her for dealing drugs, stealing from him, and vandalizing his house. Of course she had done nothing of the sort, but dealing with the hassle of it all ate her small paycheck and had caused her to lose two other jobs. In his latest move, he'd stolen her cats.

She'd only started working at the club a few weeks ago, but once Stacey learned of her plight, she decided that she needed to do something about it, which meant *we* needed to do something about it. We were the sort of friends that if you called one of us to say you'd killed someone, we'd show up with shovels and an alibi and no questions asked.

When the waitress—I think her name was Lydia—

showed up one day with bruises, that had been the last straw. Stacey was not one to stand by and watch somebody get abused. None of us were. We decided to rescue the cats, teach the ex a lesson, and make sure he never hurt anybody again. What kind of psychopath steals cats anyway? Or any pets at all? That's ninth circle of hell shit right there.

Lydia, of course, had no idea what we were up to, or she'd try to stop us for fear of backlash. The asshole ex—Carson Flannery—had convinced her she was helpless against him. He'd married her to be a trophy wife, and when she wasn't the meek, obedient plastic wife he'd thought he'd married, he'd taken to punishing her, and then ruining her life when she left.

He had plenty of money, a slick job, was well connected, and had a stellar reputation amongst the elite of the town, so he could get away with just about anything. I had every intention of ruining all that for him, and turning him into a cautionary tale of what can happen when you act like a dick and karma comes calling.

Just before I left to meet Jen, I got a text from Damon telling me he'd landed safely. That's it. I stared at the screen for a minute, wondering how to respond. Petty Beck wanted to say something passive aggressive like *thanks for the update. Appreciate all that detail.* Reasonable Beck actually wanted to say something similar, but I settled for *That's good. Be safe.*

*I'll call you later.*

How much later? And why not now? I rolled my eyes at myself. Apparently, I was twenty-seven going on sixteen with a bunch of hormones clogging up my brain.

*I'm not going anywhere.* I eyed the words and shrugged. He could handle the truth, and if he did call later and I didn't have my phone to answer, he might worry. I tapped out another couple of sentences. *Except maybe jail. Wish me luck.*

Jen and I sat in the back corner of the club where Stacey worked. I'd cast a little bubble to dull the sound of the pounding dance music, so that we could talk without shouting ourselves hoarse. Before meeting her, I'd dropped Ajax off with Lorraine. If we got arrested, I wanted to know he was safe. He hadn't been happy about my desertion, but he liked Lorraine and had finally agreed to stay.

Jen and I were dressed nearly identically, except she looked badass, while I looked like I'd failed goth class. Jen always reminded me of an Amazon. Sure, she looked the part with her six foot height, waist-length, black-coffee hair, and her naturally tanned skin, but what made her Amazonian in my head was the way she always seemed in control of every situation. Nothing surprised her and nobody scared her, even when she should be. She's tough as proverbial nails and that's why I made sure she never knew what Aunty Mommy was up to, and why I did my best to keep them separated. In a fair fight, I'd have bet on Jen, but Aunty Mommy never played fair, and she was both sadistic and a witch. It still terrifies me to think what she might have done.

Earlier, we'd opted not to eat dinner but take a walk along the river. Instead, we'd ordered fried dill pickles, onion rings, and deep fried cheese sticks, all of which were now gone, and now sipped our drinks. Iced tea for me, soda for her. I'd run over the events in Sutton earlier in the day and the warning that Lindsey had given me.

"The ghost *bit* you?"

I grimaced and pointed at the bandage. "Yep."

"That's fucked-up bizarro. Is that a ghost thing or just a bitch thing?"

"Don't know about the ghost, but definitely yes on the bitch," I replied. "I might have to have Lorraine give me a rabies shot."

Jen shook her head in silent disbelief. "Biting aside, I don't like how vague that warning is about something bad's coming for you," she said, drumming her fingers on the table. "That leaves a lot of open territory. And what's the definition of bad? Your fake mom was serial killer bad. Is that better or worse than what your psychic friend saw?"

I shrugged. "Good questions. I have no idea. For all I know, it means I'm going to get a speeding ticket, or maybe a giant zit on the end of my nose."

"On the other hand, given our plans for tonight, it could mean something a lot more serious."

"True. It could also have nothing to do with tonight, and whatever bad thing she's talking about might not happen for twenty more years."

Jen nodded with a grimace.

"Annoying to know something's coming but not when, where, how, or why, or how bad. There are a billion possibilities."

I nodded, stirring the ice in my tea with my straw.

"Are you going to go see Lindsey again? See if she knows anything else?"

"Rhi and Lorel said it could take days for her to recover. I'll probably call next week to see how she's doing and go from there."

"You think they've got enough left to have a sale?"

"Doubt it. There may be some things left I could do on

consignment, but really most of the stock is trashed, and I doubt that Mitzi's apartment will offer much to the high-end buyer. They'll be better selling on Craigslist or eBay, or maybe having a garage sale. Maybe hiring a different sales company. Chandeliers could be valuable. I'd need to take a closer look. And there's potential in the psychic reading room."

"At least you took their wicked witch out of the equation," Jen said. She lifted her glass in a silent toast. "Maybe you should add that to your services."

"I'm guessing hit-woman-for-hire is more up your alley than mine."

"Can't argue. Though I'm more of a hacker-hitter. Stacey, now, she could shiv a guy in the heart while fucking him. *And* she'd get an orgasm or two in first."

"But that would mean taking on targets worth fucking," I pointed out. "Can you make a living killing only hand-some, muscular men?"

"Too bad she's not bi. That would extend her potential revenue quite a bit."

"Yeah, except she wouldn't murder people who didn't deserve it, and how do you even advertise that kind of business?"

Jen shrugged. "I could set her up on the dark web. Wouldn't be that hard. Wouldn't have to kill everybody, either. She could offer maiming and torturing services. Her motto could be: Go ahead and get mad, then get even. Revenge for hire."

I grinned. "That totally sounds like her. She'll be so excited to hear we've planned her new career path."

"Uh oh," Jen said, her gaze sliding past me. "Look what the cat dragged in."

I turned to look.

The man in question stood a couple inches over six feet. His gray cowboy boots pushed him up taller. Black jeans wrapped his legs like lover's hands, and made his ass look mouthwatering. His shoulders were wide, his waist lean, his forearms ropey with muscle where they emerged from a dove gray western shirt with pearl buttons. He walked upright with his shoulders squared like he was ready for a fight. His brown hair bristled from his head in a short, military-style cut. His square jaw was clean-shaven, showing off his all-American good looks.

"Well, fuck. Just what we needed when we're planning to go out criming," I said.

"He sure is pretty, though. Wonder if he's got back hair."

I eyed her. "Back hair? Tell me that's not a turn-on."

Jen grinned. "Exactly. I'd hate to think he was a perfect specimen of virile manhood. Not when he's such a holier-than-thou prick."

"Maybe he's compensating for his small dick."

"Guess we'll never know," she said, leaning back in her chair to watch him.

Mike Crowe—Officer Mike Crowe—had been trying to get Stacey into a wedding ring for a couple of years now. Never going to happen. Stacey had no intention of following the bad example of her parents and all their steps into marriage. Between her father and mother, they'd had nine weddings. Stacey's mother remained married to her fourth husband, though the way things were going that could change any day now, and her father was trolling for his sixth wife, having finalized his latest divorce a few months back.

Her parents, however, remained friends with each other and all their other spouses. Though Stacey was their only child together, they each had three or four more biological children with other people, plus a couple dozen step children, if you counted all the kids their other spouses had, which they did. Stacey's family was like the mafia: once you were in, you could never get out.

The whole situation was an Elmore Leonard book waiting to happen. Stacey had decided long ago she'd have to get a lobotomy to want to get married. She'd been excited when Officer Hotpants, as she'd dubbed him, invited her out. Two dates later and he'd turned into Officer Stick-Up-His-Ass, and she'd dropped him like a bad habit.

The problem was she was most men's wet dream. Petite with blonde ringlets, a curvy figure, and a bright smile, she looked like a sexy angel, a fact she wasn't oblivious to and often took advantage of.

She continued to flirt outrageously with Officer Obnoxiously-Hot but had told him in no uncertain terms that she'd fuck him but not marry him. Clearly he didn't quite believe her. Or maybe the flirting gave him hope. I'll admit I took great satisfaction in knowing that he went home with blue balls every time he saw her.

My malice was justified. Officer My-Shit-Don't-Stink despised me, Lorraine, and Jen. He'd developed the bizarre belief that Stacey would be pure as the driven snow if not for us. The fact that she wasn't interested in any long term commitments or settling down was apparently our fault, because we'd infected her with slut cooties or something.

As if.

I was still mostly a virgin. Lorraine rarely had time for lovers, even one night stands. Jen couldn't be bothered by most men she met. Stacey was the free spirit, encouraging all of us to enjoy ourselves, even temporarily. Officer Blue-

Balls would probably have a heart attack if he got a look at her toy drawer.

He strode through the rambunctious crowd like he was on a mission, dodging dancers and waitstaff and ignoring all the admiring stares he was getting from women and men alike. He took a seat at the bar and waited for Stacey to notice him. The club was hopping, crowded more than usual for Thursday night. Even with two other bartenders, Stacey could hardly keep up.

Eventually she saw him. She gave him a bright smile and a wave, then filled a frosty-cold glass with dark beer and set it before him. Ignoring the clamors for her attention from thirsty customers, she gripped the brass bar rail and hoisted herself up off her feet, leaning forward so she could get close enough for him to hear her. He bent and met her half way, listening intently.

She spoke for a few moments and dropped back to the floor, waiting for him to reply. He stared, his expression startled and then disappointed, before giving a slight nod. She flashed him another sunny smile and hurried back to work.

"Wonder what that was about," I said.

"Talk about an inconvenient time for Mikey to show up," Jen said. "Hopefully she was telling him to get lost before he gets in the way."

"If he gets in the way, I'll just flatten all his tires," I said.

Jen glanced back at him and scowled. "Oh, for fuck's sake. He's headed over here. Quick! Tie his shoes together, or better yet, turn him into a toad."

"He's wearing cowboy boots, and people would probably panic if he suddenly turned into a toad," I said, after a moment's contemplation. "Wouldn't want to be responsible for the injuries when they stampeded out of here."

"Then glue his boots to the floor. Or put cockroaches in his pants."

My brows rose. "Not bees? Or spiders?"

"Or all three."

"I'd have thought you'd be itching to tell him off."

"I'd love to kick him in the balls, but Stacey wouldn't appreciate me getting arrested before we actually go commit tonight's crimes," Jen said, watching Officer Asswipe weave his way through the club's boisterous crowd.

"True."

"Anyway, she does like him. Apparently, he can be smart and funny when he's not a jackass."

From the way he walked, it was clear we were his destination. Not that he seemed happy about it. His chill gaze swept over us, and he got a look on his face like he'd eaten a rotten egg. Without a word, he slid into the booth, sandwiching me between Jen and him. We both gave him a *what the fuck* look.

"Didn't anybody teach you that you're supposed to ask before you make yourself at home at someone else's table?" Jen asked.

"Stacey sent me over, so you can take it up with her," he replied in a delicious, hot-silk voice that was made to talk women out of their panties. Of course, once you knew he was a self-righteous prick, it was easy enough to resist. All the same, I had to wonder how often women spontaneously orgasmed when he was giving them a speeding ticket.

"Stacey? She sent you over *here*?" she repeated. "Are you sure she didn't tell you to go to hell?"

He gave her a cold look. "If so, it appears I've arrived."

I looked at Jen. "I don't think Mikey likes us."

She was in the middle of drinking her soda and snorted liquid out her nose as she broke out laughing.

After gaining control and wiping her face with her cocktail napkin, she poked me in the shoulder. "Why do you suppose Stacey would send him our way? I know she likes us, so it can't be the torture factor."

"She needed a chance to breathe? He sucks a lot of the air out of the room," I suggested.

"Stacey invited me here tonight," he said easily. "Looks like you got the same invite. Question is, why do you both look like you got dressed in the dark? I'm surprised the bouncers let you in."

"What, you haven't heard of thrift store goth chic?" Jen said with a perfectly straight face.

We were both dressed alike; dark jeans, dark shirts, and had our hair pulled back in pony tails. Jen wore a pair of scuffed Doc Martens. Not exactly club attire.

"Thrift store goth chic?" He echoed brows shooting up. "That's what you're going with?"

"Is it better to look like you're on your way to a rodeo?" Jen looked around. "We blend in better than you."

"And blending is good?"

Officer Howdy-Pilgrim might be a better cop than we wanted to give him credit for. At least he stayed focused *and* was getting us to talk.

"Whatever bullshit you have planned, keep Stacey out of it."

Or maybe not.

I snorted. "*We* haven't planned a damned thing. Like you said, we were invited, just like you, though why she wants you involved, I haven't a clue." I glanced at Jen. "If I ever need a cop, don't call him. I want one with at least half a brain."

"I'm beginning to wonder if Stacey has a tumor that's keeping her from kicking Officer Mikey here to the curb. Or maybe he's dying, and she's taken pity on him. There's got to be *some* reason she lets him hang around. We know it's not for the hot sex."

Mikey flushed, his jaw hardening. Guess that struck a nerve.

"Why is it women always get blamed for believing they can change men, when men do it just as much, if not more? You'd think this jackass would want Stacey any way he could get her, but no, she's not good enough for Sir Galahad the Prude. Talk about weapons-grade stupid. I'm surprised she bothers with him."

"Like I said, maybe it's a tumor."

Jen didn't respond. She was on a roll. "And he has the gall to think we are bad friends when we're willing to hide the bodies, no questions asked. That's the definition of a good friend. I swear, you should have gone the cockroach route when you had a chance."

I cocked my head and considered Officer Peckersnot. "There's still time."

He curled his lip. "I've heard enough about your exploits to know Stacey would be better off without you dragging her into trouble. If you cared about her the way you say you do, you'd back off before you get her involved in something that lands her in jail."

I barely resisted the urge to dump my tea all over him. Talk about arrogant.

Despite Aunty Mommy's malicious efforts at getting rid of my girls, neither Lorraine, Stacey, or Jen ever thought about deserting me, even when I tried to push them away for their own good. The four of us had been through hell together. We'd die for each other; we'd bury bodies for each other. We were fucking family. Who did Officer Buttbreath think he was, to want to kick us out of Stacey's life?

I practically snarled. "What could you possibly know about the four of us?"

"She told me about what you four did on your mother's grave. If you'd been caught, all four of you would have been up on charges. Far as I can tell, you've been getting into trouble for most of your lives and dragging Stacey into it."

My anger pegged in the red. My hands tightened into fists, my knuckles whitening as I tried to reel myself in. His accusation shouldn't have pissed me off this bad, but this wasn't about what he'd said, exactly. It was about Aunty Mommy and all the times she'd tried to drive the girls off, and how they never gave up on me. I'd done everything I could to protect them; I'd submitted to Aunty Mommy's torture to protect them. And now this fucker had the nerve to accuse me of *hurting* Stacey?

I drew a breath and let it out, told myself to let it go. He didn't matter. If I looked at him, I'd rip his head off, so I kept my gaze fixed on my glass. A minute passed. Before I was ready, he jumped on my silence.

"You're not arguing," he said. "You know I'm right."

My brain short circuited and my mouth switched to autopilot. "On the contrary. I was making an effort to be calm and not rip your vocal cords out with my fingers. But let me see if I understand. You want the three of us to bail on Stacey, at which point you could step in and fill the void we leave behind, right?" I put on a confused face. "Isn't that how abuse works? Isolate the victim from her friends, start telling her who she can talk to, maybe start slapping her around when she won't obey? Out of curiosity, did you go to cop school to get tips on being a domestic abuser?"

His face clouded and red stained his cheeks. I didn't let

him say a word.

"We're her *family,* you pretentious little prick, and you can damned well be sure we'll be in her life long after you're just a bad memory. You're just some random dirtbag who thinks he knows what's better for her than she does, so you try to run her life. Not only that, you do your dirty work behind her back. I'm fucking done sharing air with you."

I needed out of that booth like I needed oxygen. If I stayed, I was going to do something I probably wouldn't regret but definitely should.

Thought didn't enter into what I did next. Pure instinct and knowledge that came straight out of my genes guided me. In the blink of an eye I turned into smoke and swirled to the open side of the booth before solidifying back into myself. I had no idea how I did it, just that it generally happened in moments of strong emotion when I couldn't otherwise escape.

I'd never done it in front of anybody but Damon, back when he was trying to kidnap me. Jen's eyes widened, and she looked utterly delighted. Meanwhile, Sergeant My-Shit-Don't-Stink's expression went from confused to bewildered and then ice-cold, his body coiling tight.

"How the fuck did you do that?" he demanded as he stood.

"Duh. Magic," Jen said, as if that was a reasonable conclusion. Which, to be fair, it was, but since magic wasn't supposed to be real, not the likeliest conclusion for anybody who hadn't experienced it.

"I wasn't talking to you," he snapped and focused back on me. "How did you do that?"

I folded my arms, my chin jutting. I could have tried to cool things down, but why? Escalation was fine by me.

"Is it just impossible for you to believe the truth when it

comes from a woman? *It's magic.*" I then used said magic to shove him back down into his seat without moving a single muscle.

His mouth dropped open, and his eyes widened. His gaze locked on me in the same way he might look at an armed and dangerous suspect. At least he was smart enough to figure that out.

"*What the fuck are you?*"

I rolled my eyes and snapped my fingers in front of him. "Focus, Mister Policeman. We're not talking about me; we're talking about how you can cure your asshole disease."

He knocked my hand aside. "Magic isn't real."

"No? Then explain what I did."

"You did something to hypnotize me."

"Yep. I totally hypnotized you." I waggled my fingers in the air in front of him. "You're getting sleeeeepy...."

Jen laughed and he shot her an annoyed look, his attention snapping instantly back to me as if he was afraid I'd do something in the split second he turned away.

"Oh! I've got it," I said. "I'm bionic. I'm a super secret government experiment. Or no! A mutant with superpowers! I'm a super villain. Quick, Jen, what's my super villain name?"

"Razor Bitch? Iced Vengeance? No Fucks Left? Queen of the Night?"

"If it isn't two of my favorite ladies."

The husky male voice spun me around. Luke Galloway —Stacey's tall, dark, gorgeous, and very slutty stepbrother —gave me a shit-eating grin and a flirtatious wink.

I rolled my eyes. Just what I didn't need. Super Slutman. Now that was a super-villain name.

"You look good enough to eat," he said, sliding an arm

around my waist and pulling me against him.

His hand drifted lower. I grabbed it and twisted. He yelped and jerked away.

"Jesus, Beck! You don't have to break my hand." He flexed it and winced.

"Don't worry," Jen said. "You can still beat off with the other."

He chuckled and shoved her over, wrapping his arm around her shoulders.

"If you want to keep that arm, you should back the fuck off," Jen said, giving him the side-eye.

Luke lifted the offending limb away. "Can't blame a guy for trying."

Jen gave an impatient sigh. "You try every time we're in the same room together. I don't even think you're interested. It's just a habit."

He shrugged. "I'm always interested. You could change your mind. Women are fickle. You know I'd show you a seriously good time." He smiled with the confidence of a man who knew he was good in the sack.

"Your offers might work better if you weren't also trying to pick up every other woman in the room."

"Not every one. Just the interesting ones."

"Bitch, please. Interesting in your world translates into 'has a hole for your dick.'" I put air quotes around 'interesting.' "You'd fuck a pumpkin if it was handy."

Jen snorted soda out her nose again, grabbing my cocktail napkin and wiping her face. "You could warn a girl," she told me, sniffing and rubbing tears from her eyes.

I made a face. "It's not like I think before I speak."

"True enough. What are you doing here?" She asked Luke. "Didn't Stacey forbid you from coming here? Something about not wanting to clean up after your romantic encounters? And by romantic, I mean fucking everything that moves."

"She did. Unfairly, too. I mean, my lovers always leave satisfied," he said in a wounded voice.

"So why are you here?"

"Stacey told me to be."

Officer Meathead *and* Luke? What was Stacey thinking?

During this entire exchange, Sergeant Mike had continued to watch me through narrowed eyes, his mouth flat.

"Who's the stiff?" Luke asked, nudging his chin at the other man.

"You don't know each other?" I asked, surprised.

"That's gotta be a hate crime. You two have *so* much to talk about," Jen said with a wicked grin.

"Let me introduce you," I said, proceeding to throw napalm on the burgeoning fire. "Luke, meet Sergeant Mike Crowe. He believes me, Jen, and Lorraine, are a terrible influence on poor, innocent, virginal Stacey. He thinks she should drop us like a bad habit. He'd like nothing more than to drag her off to a church and then to his cave where he can keep Stacey barefoot and pregnant. Sergeant Mikey, this is Luke Galloway, Stacey's stepbrother who's been trying to get into her pants since the day they met. He would like to drag her back to his sex dungeon and fuck her blind."

The two men eyed one another. Luke looked almost sleepy, but I could see a surprisingly sharp flash of emotion in his gray eyes. Sergeant Mike, on the other hand, looked like he wouldn't mind putting a bullet in Luke's head.

Jen pulled out her phone to record the moment for posterity, Stacey, and Lorraine.

Sergeant Mikey lobbed the first shot over the bow.

"What kind of man wants to sleep with his sister?"

Luke kicked back and casually crossed his ankles under the table, giving every indication that he was relaxed and maybe a little bored.

"Stepsister," he said finally. "Shouldn't a cop at least try to get the details right? Or maybe you're just piss-poor at your job."

Mikey's lip curled and his eyes narrowed. He looked lethal. Dangerous. Bad boy. Stacey always did like a good bad boy. Unfortunately, Sergeant Mikey was actually a boy scout.

"Does it matter? You want to fuck your sister."

Luke's mouth curved slightly. "When my father married her mother, I was twenty-two and Stacey was eighteen. She's no more my sister than Jen or Beck. Our parents divorced about ten minutes after the wedding, so we're not even related on paper." He glanced over at me. "By the way, I like to think of it as a playroom, not a dungeon." He winked.

I couldn't help myself. I grinned. "I stand corrected. My apologies."

"She's too good for you," Mikey practically growled. His jaw had tightened so hard I thought he might break teeth.

"Undoubtedly," Luke agreed. "Doesn't mean I can't make her feel very *very* good. I bet you're one of those missionary men who doesn't know how to spell clitoris, much less find it. I'm a full service lover. I make sure it's an orgasmic experience for all involved. I'd work extra hard for Stacey."

Mikey flushed, but before he could speak, the music died and a brass bell clanged. Someone hollered last call. I checked the time on my phone. Almost one. Stacey would get off at two.

Once upon a time she'd have had another hour or two of cleaning left, but not any more. For months the other employees had taken advantage of her relentless sense of responsibility and started leaving her to clean and restock by herself. When she'd complained, management ignored her. When she'd quit, management suddenly grew a brain and upped her wages and made her bar manager, as well as releasing her from cleanup responsibilities.

As the echoes of the bell faded and the music erupted again, Luke abruptly stood and held out a hand to Jen. "Let's dance."

Jen considered and then shrugged, allowing him to help her up. With a not-terribly-apologetic grimace at me, she disappeared into the crowd on the dance floor. I settled into Jen's vacated seat. Officer Mikey studied me while I pretended to ignore him.

"Maybe we should get to know each other."

"I know enough, thank you."

"You don't know a damned thing about me."

I snorted. "You do realize Stacey talks to us, don't you?"

"You're saying she doesn't have a high opinion of me."

"I'm the one who doesn't have a high opinion of you. Well, Jen and Lorraine, too. Stacey simply knows the two of you aren't compatible, so she's not going to waste time and emotion getting involved with someone who's clearly a dead-end."

"And if I don't want to be a dead-end?" Mikey waved to get the attention of the passing waiter.

He set a couple of clean cocktail napkins down and picked up the empty beer bottle, setting it on his round, cork-lined tray. "What can I get for you?"

"Another beer and whatever those are." Mikey gestured toward Jen's and my glasses.

"Ice tea," I said when the waiter looked the question at me. "And Coke."

He nodded and hurried away. Mikey watched him go and then turned back to me.

"If I don't want it to be a dead-end?" he repeated.

"That sucks, but you want someone she's not. Story ends before it begins. Move on."

He scraped his teeth over his lip, thinking. He seemed to come to a conclusion. "I was in a serious relationship once."

I waited, but that seemed to be all he planned to say. "That's…nice?" I said. "Not sure what your point is."

The corner of his mouth kicked up. The waiter returned and set our drinks down. Mikey dug out his wallet and handed the other man some cash. "Keep the change."

Mikey took a drink and set the bottle down, turning it in his fingers. "I was all in, and it turns out she wasn't. I promised myself I'd learn my lesson. I wouldn't let anything like that happen again. Instead, I focused on work. Got promoted." A grimace and shake of his head. "Then I met Stacey."

"I fought the attraction hard, but…." He blew out a breath. "I can't seem to stay away from her." He paused. "I want forever. Why is that so god-damned wrong?"

He shot an angry look at me. Like I was to blame.

"It's not wrong." I thought of Damon. I was the skittish one, trying to figure out how I felt and what I wanted. I couldn't really blame Mikey for knowing what he wanted and going after it. Not his fault Stacey was more than a little leery of marriage. She'd seen the absolute worst of it with her revolving door of step parents. She trusted marriage vows as much as she trusted the ingredient list on a log of bologna. "But it's also not Stacey's fault she doesn't want what you want."

Actually, the truth was Stacey did want long-term. She did want commitment. She just didn't believe either was actually possible. I had no intention of sharing that with him.

"What should I do?"

My eyes just about popped out of my head. "Excuse me?"

He smiled. "I'm desperate."

"You'd have to be."

He eyed me expectantly. Did he have his gun on him? Maybe I could put myself out of my misery.

"A half hour ago you despised me, thought I was a terrible influence, and wanted me out of Stacey's life. Now you suddenly want my advice? Don't you think that's a) asinine, b) hypocritical as fuck, and c) ridiculous? Or is it just a pathetic attempt at sucking up? Also, why me?"

He grimaced. Unexpected humor lit his brown eyes. "I can count on you to be honest," he said wryly. "I think Jen would make up lies just to get me in trouble."

He was totally right about both of us. Maybe he was a better cop than I'd given him credit for.

"That doesn't mean I want to help you, and anyway, you already know what you need to do. You just don't want to."

"And what's that?" He took a swig from his bottle, never taking his eyes off me.

That skewering stare was getting annoying, but if he thought it would intimidate me, he had a lot to learn. I'd faced down the worst monster anybody could dream up, and while she'd broken me physically more times than I could count, she'd never made me submit mentally.

"Loosen the fuck up and get over your bad self. Take what you can get and be happy about it. Maybe it'll last, and maybe it won't, but at least you'll have had a great ride while it lasts. You also might want to reevaluate the wisdom of crapping all over her best friends. Not exactly a winning strategy."

He winced. "Sorry."

"Say that again later when you don't want something from me."

"I guess I deserve that."

I rolled my eyes. "You think?"

"Are you going to sabotage me with Stacey?"

"I thought we covered this; Stacey does what she wants to do."

"But you're her friend, and she listens to you—to all three of you."

I laughed. "You're wishing you'd been less of an ass, aren't you?"

"More tactful, anyhow," he agreed. He took a moment to consider his beer thoughtfully before taking a slow drink.

Because I knew what was coming before he even opened his mouth, I gave the answer he didn't want to accept. "Magic."

I flicked a little ball of light off my fingers. It looped around the top of his bottle before sliding down inside, where it continued to bounce around. "There's some proof for you. If you want more, I'd be more than happy to turn your underwear into a swarm of cockroaches. Or spiders. Or potato bugs. Those things are creepy as fuck. Think about it. I'm going to go dance."

I walked away.

# CHAPTER SIX

The whole plan went to hell in the blink of an eye. Not that I knew what the plan was, just that Stacey had one.

I'd followed Jen and Luke back to the table and was just sitting down when I got a text, and then four more. Each contained a picture of a ledger filled in with tiny, crabbed writing, the last ripped across the top. Frowning, I zoomed in to see better. My chest knotted as I started reading.

Each page contained fifty or sixty entries, though I couldn't read them. They were in some kind of code with a lot of abbreviations and little pictures, like hieroglyphs. The expense and debit columns contained positive and negative numbers ranging from one to five, with a total recorded at the bottom. Someone had highlighted the headings of each page. They all said the same thing: *Anne Wyatt: Business Exchanges Chronicled and Tabulated.*

Anne Wyatt. Aunty Mommy. My aunt and the woman who'd kidnapped and tortured me most of my life.

"What the fuck?"

I scanned the pages again and checked the number

they'd come from before typing out a response: who are you?

But even as I hit send, another text popped up: *We found these. Lindsey woke up and says you need to come now. It's important. You can do the other thing tomorrow. The asshole's having a garden party. You'll be able to walk in without any challenges.*

Another text hard on the heels of that one: *This is Rhi.*

"Beck? What's going on? You look like you just got hit by a bus."

I lifted my eyes from my phone and met Jen's concerned gaze. "I'm not sure. Have a look."

I passed her my phone and wrapped my arms around my stomach, my fingers digging hard into the flesh just above my elbows. Aunty Mommy might not be hanging around as a ghost, but she definitely wasn't entirely gone.

Jen gave a silent whistle as she scrolled through the pictures.

"Garden party? Is she talking about Lydia's ex?"

"Think so."

"You believe her? Think she really is psychic?"

"Psychic?" Luke and Mikey echoed at the same time.

I nodded at Jen, ignoring the two men. "I do."

She'd scanned through the documents, her brow furrowing. "What do the entries even mean? And what kind of business would your aunt be doing with this Mitzi bitch?"

"Fuck if I know, but it can't be good. Mixing Mitzi and Aunty Mommy would be a cocktail of napalm and agent orange with a chaser of nuclear waste."

"Why do they think Lindsey wants to see you right now? Is it related to that bad thing she predicted?"

"Who the fuck knows?" But I'd taken back my phone and tapped out the question.

"Bad thing?" Luke said. "Can someone explain what the fuck you're talking about? I feel like I'm in the Twilight Zone."

"Hush," Jen said. "Let the grownups talk."

Rhi replied to my text almost instantly. *I don't know, but please hurry. Lindsey's in a state, and I'm afraid she could have a heart attack or something if she doesn't see you soon. We're at the shop.*

I showed Jen the message. "I've seen her when Lindsey has a vision. It really is scary. Rhi and Lorel have to be crazy worried. I'd better go."

"I'm coming with you. Give me a minute to grab Stacey." Jen slid away through the crowd.

I glanced at my watch. Stacey's shift wasn't over, but she wouldn't care. She'd drop everything and come instantly.

"Are you going to explain what's going on now?" Luke asked, dark brows arched. "What's this shit about psychics?"

"A psychic I recently met is having a vision and wants to see me," I said, as I typed a text telling Rhi I'd be there as soon as I could.

"Seriously? You believe in that shit?" Luke asked incredulously.

"Not only that, I believe in ghosts and witches." I winked at him. Mostly to fuck with him. Now he wouldn't know if I was serious or not.

"Is there a problem?" Mikey asked, his gaze calculating. He'd morphed into cop mode, but surprisingly, didn't have the disdainful look I half expected to see. Maybe he was figuring out magic was real, and therefore had to entertain the possibility that psychics could be real too.

"I guess I'll find out when I get there."

"It's one in the morning," Mikey pointed out.

Irritation flashed through me. "Congratulations on learning to tell time, only you got it wrong; it's only midnight thirty."

He ignored my sarcasm. "Just saying it's late. Most things can wait until morning, unless it's an emergency."

"Your point?"

"If you're willing to cancel your plans and hightail it over to see them, I'm wondering just how dangerous the situation might be." Steel glinted in his eye.

"Down, boy. We're probably just talking, but even if not, I won't let anything happen to Stacey. Or Jen, for that matter. I've been protecting them for as long as I've known them."

"What about you?" He shot back.

"What about me?"

"Who's going to make sure nothing happens to you?"

That almost made my eyes pop out of my head. "Maybe if you're lucky, I'll fall in a deep hole, and you'll only have Lorraine and Jen left to contend with."

He frowned. "I'm serious."

Sure he was. I just shrugged. Anyway, if I could take care of Jen and Stacey, I could take care of myself.

"I swear to God if someone doesn't tell me what's going on, my head's going to explode," Luke said, slapping his hand on the table.

"*How* have you been protecting them?" Mikey leaned forward, studying me intently. "From what? Or who?"

Points to him for being sharp enough to think that one through.

"That's none of your business." No way was I going to tell him about life with Aunty Mommy.

"Alright. If you don't want to tell me, I'm going to come with you," he said.

"Me, too," Luke added. "Wherever the hell you're going."

I glared. "Who said either one of you is invited?

"I did," Mikey said.

The temptation to tell him to fuck off and tie him up in magic whispered a siren song in my ear. I bit the inside of my cheek until I tasted blood. I knew, in no uncertain terms, that if I did that, I was no better than Aunty Mommy. I considered that grotesque revelation. Was it true?

I wasn't prepared to answer that. Nor did I have time to think about the ethics of magic and using it for my own selfish purposes with absolutely no actual consequences. Well, except for self-loathing and disgust.

I hadn't really thought about it before. When Aunty Mommy was alive, I'd hidden my magic, only to find out after her death that she'd known all along. I'd felt like an idiot for all of two seconds before realizing she knew a whole lot more than I did about using magic and would have really gone after Jen, Lorraine, and Stacey if I'd tried to fight back with mine. I wouldn't have been able to protect them. As it was, she'd used them as hostages against my cooperation. I let her torture me; they stayed alive and healthy.

Totally worth it.

From Mikey's slightly concerned expression, I could tell he read me like a picture book. Maybe he was even testing me. Asshole.

"I'm going to wait outside." I spun around and headed for the front doors, escaping into the balmy night air. A lot of people stood outside smoking and laughing. I crossed the parking lot to where I'd parked the Highlander. Damn, but I missed my Thunderbird.

I hopped up on the hood to wait, only to find Officer Mikey coming in for a landing, with Luke striding along behind looking both pissed and confused.

Mikey stopped in front of me, his thumbs hooking in his front pockets. If he'd looked even the slightest bit smug, I'd have kicked him in the nuts. Lucky for him, he only looked thoughtful. I waited for him to say something. He didn't speak. He apparently thought that I'd hate the silence and feel compelled to start blathering like some guilty suspect. He was wrong.

I started looking at the ledger pages on my phone, trying to decipher them. Unfortunately, Mitzi's handwriting was atrocious, and I'd never been good at Sudoku, much less the mess that was her code.

Luke wandered over to stand beside me and look over my shoulder.

"I'd sure like to know what's going on."

"I'd sure like a bucket-sized margarita. Guess neither of us are getting what we want. Shouldn't you go find yourself a hook-up for the night? You've got a club full of opportunity, and it's not going to last long. It's almost time to close. Gotta keep your dick happy, right?"

He chuckled. "I'm good. Why won't you tell me?"

I slid a glance at him. "Okay. Earlier today I helped a psychic and her cousins deal with a homicidal poltergeist. Afterward, the psychic had a vision and said something bad was coming. Before you ask, I have no idea what that means. Just a few minutes ago, one of the cousins texted me with some disturbing pictures and told me I needed to come right away. Lindsey—the psychic—had another vision. There. Now you're pretty much caught up. If you have questions, keep them to yourself."

I shot a glare at Mikey, who'd obviously been listening in, and then went back to my phone.

Luke remained silent. Hallelujah. As far as I knew, the only way to shut him up was to put a tit in his mouth, or a cock or pussy, or maybe a ball-gag. Maybe I should start carrying one of the last in my purse for those 'just in case' moments, along with hand sanitizer, ChapStick, and Band-Aids.

After a moment, he leaned into me and rested his chin on my shoulder as he also looked at my phone.

"Those the pictures?"

I sighed. So much for not asking questions. "Yes."

"Looks like gibberish. What's all that mean?"

"Honestly, I have no idea. All I can say for sure is that Mitzi—the poltergeist—and my Aunty Mommy, did business together."

He lifted his head and put an arm around my shoulders and squeezed, then instantly let go as if worried I'd jab him in the stomach with my elbow. He wasn't wrong. "Stacey told me a little about your bitch of an aunt and what she did to you."

"Yeah?" I doubted she'd told him any of the really bad stuff, but the not-so-bad was plenty terrible.

"She was seriously twisted."

"Won't argue with that."

He bumped his shoulder against my arm. "Sorry. I know Stacey didn't tell me the whole story or even much of it, but you didn't deserve any of the shit she put you through."

I knew that. Most of the time, anyhow, but it was nice to hear someone else say it, especially someone who had something of an unbiased point of view.

"Thanks."

"What are you all doing out here?" Jen demanded as she and Stacey strode up.

Stacey sparkled. Rhinestones trailed across her cheekbones and made little curls on her temples. She wore high-top purple Chucks decked out with rhinestones and rainbow LED lights. Fishnet stockings woven with silver thread wrapped her legs up to her miniskirt, which was neon pink trimmed with more rhinestones, with a blue tank top and a rhinestone-studded jacket.

I hopped down off the car and hugged her hello. She smelled of alcohol and the industrial soap she used behind the bar, plus her favorite floral scent.

"You okay?" she asked, holding my arms as she stood back to examine me.

"Why wouldn't I be?"

"Jen said you caught a ghost that was trying to kill you, and that a psychic warned you about something bad happening."

"I'm fine."

"You're not hurt?"

I sighed again. End up nearly dead in the hospital a few times, and suddenly your friends think you're fragile.

"Not a scratch except for a bite, but I'm sure Jen told you about that."

She nodded, accepting my assurance. Now that Aunty Mommy and all her threats were gone, I'd promised not to withhold any information or lie to them ever again. I'd done both to protect them, and they'd forgiven me, but not again. All the truth, nothing but the truth, forever and ever, amen.

"A ghost bit you?" Mikey echoed in disbelief, his gaze dropping to the bandage on my arm.

I didn't bother to respond.

Stacey dropped my arms and glanced at our companions. "Why are we standing around? Don't we have somewhere to be?" She brushed past Luke and opened the front passenger seat.

Jen climbed in the back, and I headed for the driver's side. Next thing I know, we're out on the road, with Luke jammed between Jen and Officer Mikey in the back seat, and Stacey riding shotgun. I could have pointed out there was a third seat in the back we could fold out, but decided Mikey's disgruntled expression was too entertaining for that. Luke couldn't have been happier.

"I'm starved. Can we grab a burger or tacos or something?" Stacey asked plaintively before we'd gone a mile. "Marco stays open late for the after-hours crowd."

"You got it," I said, feeling hungry as well.

I pulled into the strip mall parking lot where Marco parked his truck on weekend nights. He served a mix of Cuban and Mexican foods, with a little bit of TexMex thrown in. He didn't have many customers at the moment, but I knew they'd pour in just as soon as The Starlight Club and the other local watering holes closed. Tonight a couple of other trucks had joined him, one Greek, the other Polish.

All of us jumped out and ordered, taking our food and getting back in the car. I'd ordered a burrito so that I could eat and drive. Stacey had four crunchy chicken tacos and a chicken fajita burrito. She could eat her weight and was always ravenous after work. I didn't see what everybody else got, but the car smelled delicious, and for a while, nobody spoke.

The two men had managed to shift Jen to the middle, either to buffer their manliness or keep from getting the other's cooties. Hard to say. I still didn't know why they'd decided to join us, or why we'd let them. Luke had been remarkably accepting of the psychic and ghost business.

"There's another seat in the back," I told Jen. "If you want to be more comfortable. I can pull over."

She shook her head. "We're in a hurry. Maybe on the way back."

"So let's hear the whole story," Stacey said after she'd gobbled her tacos. She sat sideways in the seat, her legs crossed, her back against the door. No seatbelt. The LEDs on her Chucks continued to flash. "Don't leave out the ghost wrangling part, either."

She gave me a questioning look to confirm that it was okay that she spoke openly in front of Luke and Mikey. Not that she hadn't let the cat out of the bag when she'd greeted me, but Jen had probably given her a quick and dirty rundown already, so she knew the men had witnessed our conversation when Rhi's texts arrived, not to mention my little disintegration act at the table.

The cat had long since shredded the bag and escaped.

After I told the story, I spent the rest of the drive to Sutton answering questions. Mikey seemed content to just listen. Shortly after I began to tell my story, Luke revealed he didn't believe anything I'd said and started ridiculing the idea of magic. I lobbed a ball of witch light at him. From then on, he just sat and stared wide-eyed at it bobbing in his cupped palms. I didn't doubt he was listening just as intently as Mikey.

Luke was a slut, but he was also smart. He made his money working at a tech company that did business for the government. Whatever he did for them, they made sure he was happy, paying him well and loading him up with a buttload of perks, including paid-for trips to fancy resorts all over the world, a Ferrari, a vacation house in Pebble Beach, and I don't even know what else.

He kept most of his wealth a secret, unless you noticed most of his clothes were handmade just for him, or if he took the Ferrari out. Most of the time he drove a pick-up truck with all the bells and whistles you could imagine. Basically, he was down to earth and not a snob about his money.

So to sum up: rich, slutty, and smart, but not snobby. He also had a sense of humor and frankly, the best thing about him was that for as long as I'd known him, he'd had Stacey's back. Sure, he wanted in her pants, but he'd never force her, and he'd also do just about anything for her. I was pretty sure he'd accepted he'd never get her into bed and flirted mostly because they both had fun with it.

Mikey, on the other hand, despite his asshole tendencies, seemed like a solid guy and smart, but he also had a judgmental streak a mile wide. Since he directed it at Stacey, Lorraine, Jen, and I, he was going to have to crawl a long way before I'd be willing to trust him. Or like him.

I parked in the same place I had before. When we reached the shop, the front door stood open, light from the chandeliers streaming out. I went inside and scanned the interior. The girls had been busy. The salvageable stuff had been moved to one side of the shop. Fat garbage bags lined the opposite wall. Several big garbage cans held broken glass, wood, nails, and other debris.

I glanced up to the chandelier where I'd attached Mitzi. Her pink quartz twitched and vibrated. Jen and Stacey followed my gaze.

"That's her?" Stacey asked.

I nodded.

"I thought my first ghost would be more interesting," she said, eyeing the crystal.

"I could let her loose, but she'd probably pull the building down on us," I said.

"You're here!" Rhi hurried in from Mitzi's psychic reading room. The relief on her face was almost painful. She waved her hand. "Come quickly. She's gotten worse."

She disappeared and I followed, the others trailing after me.

When I stepped through the heavy velvet drapes, my gaze instantly went to Lindsey. She sat in one of the chairs at the glass-and-wood pedestal table. Her head hung down, her hair hiding her face. She sat stiff in the chair, arms dangling. She still wore gloves. Her breathing wheezed loud in the little chamber, alternating with sounds that could have been whimpers.

She shuddered and her breathing stopped. Her ribs bellowed as she fought for oxygen. She threw her head back. Her eyes stared wildly at the ceiling. Her body twitched and shook, her mouth opening and closing like a fish. Sweat dampened her face and darkened her shirt. She looked like she'd been working for hours in the Arizona sun. Her skin had gone bright red, and her eyes looked bloody from popped capillaries. She didn't blink.

Lorelei stood behind her, wringing her hands as she spoke quickly into Lindsey's ear. She glanced up as I came into the room.

"She's here. Do you hear me? Beck is here. You can talk to her now. Please breathe. *Please.*"

Lindsey didn't react. I strode to her and stood over her, putting my face in her field of vision.

"Lindsey? Can you hear me? You need to breathe." And if she didn't, I'd have to do it for her. Mouth to mouth? Or using magic?

"I know CPR," Mikey volunteered.

"Same," Stacey said.

When Lindsey started to bow up out of the chair, her feet on the floor, her neck pressed against the back of the chair, I bent and grabbed her hand, stripping off the glove so I could touch her skin to skin.

A porcupine exploded in my brain. I collapsed against the table and dropped to the floor, my vision fracturing into confetti. Nothing made sense. My chest clenched down and I couldn't breathe. I fought a panic that wasn't mine. Lindsey's emotions pounded through me in a cataract of frenzied fear and desperation. I heard her screaming. That I heard her only inside my head made no difference. The sound ripped through me like I'd been hit with a taser.

Vaguely I was aware of shouting and talking and the smell of lemons and cloves. Weird. In my mind, thick clouds of greasy yellow and black smoke billowed up. I wanted to hold my breath, but that only reminded me I couldn't breathe. Prickles ran under my skin, quickly turning to pinpricks and then scraping. I twitched and shuddered, but couldn't rid myself of the sensation.

*Lindsey?* I might have said her name aloud. I wasn't sure. What I did know was that if I didn't start breathing soon, Jen and Stacey were going to kill me. *Come on, Lindsey. You wanted to talk to me. I'm here. What's going on?*

I had an impression of her searching for me, that frantic energy stirring the smoke into a bubbling churn. The greasiness stuck to me like I'd gone a week without showering and then rolled around in congealed bacon fat. Eerie noises twisted around me, like they'd been pulled out of shape. It was like being in a house of mirrors, only instead of distorting images, they distorted sound.

The feeling that I couldn't breathe grew more urgent. My eyes swelled and my heart thundered, a bass drum playing counterpoint to the weird ribbons of noise.

*Lindsey!* I put all my strength into the mental shout, then remembered I was a witch. How could I help her? She was trapped in some sort of psychic fugue, and she'd dragged me in with her.

I couldn't separate myself. I needed another psychic. Someone who could reach Lindsey and break her free. I only knew of one other, and she was as likely to help us as I was to forgive Aunty Mommy. But since I didn't have another option, I did the only thing I could: I called Mitzi's rose quartz prison to my hand.

I thought I'd have to crack her bindings, but as soon as the rock hit my palm, Lindsey yanked her into her freakout too.

I found myself face-to-face with the woman. Except she was a ghost, and this was all in my head. How that worked, I couldn't begin to fathom, nor did I care. Somebody else could explain magical physics. Right now, I only needed to know if she could help Lindsey.

Mitzi looked a lot like Rhi and Lorel. A sixty-year old version. She stood tall and slender, her hair dyed an orangey red. Her face appeared smooth, with few crow's feet or other lines. But then, most lines required you to smile or laugh. From the glacial chill of her blue eyes, I doubted she understood the concept of humor. Hate, now, that one she had an expert handle on.

Then she smiled and I realized smiles could be malicious and triumphant and didn't necessarily require humor. If she'd been wearing a fur coat or had black and white hair, I'd have called her Cruella de Vil. As it was, Charles Manson popped to mind.

"Looks like you're in a spot of trouble," she said, and her smile widened. It was a Grinch smile, exactly like in the cartoon.

"I always knew Lindsey would choke. Just like her mom. The power was wasted on them."c

It didn't take a psychic or a psychiatrist to translate that statement. Mitzi hated Lindsey and her mother because they had stronger psychic abilities than she did.

"Course you didn't bother helping either of them, did you?" I said it like I already knew the answer, which I did. Mitzi probably would have sucked a donkey's dick before she'd help them.

"Why should I? I had to learn everything myself," she snarled. "If you expect me to help her now, you're fatally wrong." Again, that fat smile. "I know who you are, you know. Your mother and I did a lot of business together."

"My aunt," I corrected. "She kidnapped me and claimed to be my mother. I wonder if the universe thought it was funny to pair up two psychopath aunts to torture the children under their power?"

"I was a wonderful mother to Lorelei and Rhiannon. Lindsey deserved nothing good from me."

"Only because you're a jealous hag who apparently cheated your own sister out of her half of this store."

I probably should have tried sucking up, since I didn't really have any way to force her to help Lindsey. Using honey rather than shit to lure her, but then maybe she liked shit. Maybe I couldn't scrape up a fuck to give.

I'd begun to feel like giant bubbles were burbling around in my head. An iron band crushed my chest. I probably should have been more worried, but both Mikey and

Stacey knew CPR, so they could keep both me and Lindsey alive for a little while, anyway.

I knew that it wasn't entirely sane of me to calmly rely on CPR to save my life, but this whole situation was insane, and I had to go with the flow. I also knew Mitzi wanted to see me panic, and I wasn't going to give her the satisfaction.

"My sister was a good-for-nothing waste of flesh. I practically had to do everything for her her entire life. She burned half her brain up when she was thirteen and never recovered. She was irresponsible and unreliable. She put money into the store, but I planned everything. I decorated, ordered stock, courted artists, and gave readings. I found your mother and she supplied me with magical talismans, curses, hexes, potions, and all kinds of artifacts."

"Aunt," I replied automatically. "And that's how you guarantee orgasms," I said as realization dawned.

She gave me an 'are you serious' look, and then nodded. "Exactly."

"So let me see if I understand. You hated your sister because she needed you, and you couldn't be bothered. You hate Lindsey because she's her mother's daughter, and you despise her for not being able to learn how to handle her psychic abilities by herself. Wasn't enough for you to make her life miserable; you died and made her your executor so you could rub her nose in all she could have had if you'd actually cared about her. You're a gold-medal bitch, aren't you?"

"Survival of the fittest," she said. "Neither Lace nor her spawn are fit enough to survive."

I wanted to punch the smugness out of her. I didn't have the time and very likely I didn't have the ability.

"Here's the situation, Mitzi. You're bound to that chunk

of quartz, and you're going to stay bound. You do have a choice, however. If you help Lindsey now and teach her what she needs to know, I'll make sure you get to enjoy your ghost-hood. You'll get to travel, or haunt people, or whatever makes your stainless steel heart happy. If you don't help, I'll put you in a lead box and wrap it so tight, you'll spend the rest of your existence in darkness and silence. What'll it be?"

"As if you'll be able to escape," she said with a sneer. "You'll no more survive than Lindsey will."

"If you want to bet your future on that, go ahead, but you're risking spending eternity in a black box with only yourself for company. No music, no conversation, no window into the world, just you with your miserable thoughts. Are you willing to take that chance, just so you can continue your petty crusade against your niece? Against a woman who doesn't deserve it?"

I could feel her wrestling with herself. At the same time, I felt air pushing into my lungs and the dull numbness that had begun to swallow me retreated.

"Tick tock, Mitzi. All deals go *poof!* Once Lindsey figures out how to pull out of this. When she does, that's the end of any leverage you have. I should probably tell you that the one thing I shared with my aunt is a powerful vindictive streak. I'll put your box on my mantle and take enormous delight in knowing you're suffering the way you made Lindsey suffer all these years. In fact, please don't take the deal. I'm looking forward to making your death a nightmare. Given a few minutes, I know I can think up even more creative ways to fuck with you."

It was my turn for the Grinch grin as I felt her quail, and then her surrender.

"Very well," she said. "I will do as you say."

With that, she walked into the boiling black and yellow clouds, making an expression of distaste as she went.

I couldn't hear what she said to Lindsey, and I had no idea how long she'd been gone, but a sledgehammer clobbered my brain and that was all I knew.

When I woke up, I found myself staring up into Stacey's angry blue eyes. I blinked, my own eyes feeling gritty and dry.

"Hey."

The single word sent fire rolling around my ribs. I sucked in a breath, which only served to increase the pain. I coughed in reaction and my pain skyrocketed.

"Here. Drink."

Jen cupped the back of my head, helping me sit up a little as she pressed a glass of water to my lips. I sipped, and sipped again, then grabbed the glass and guzzled. My entire body felt parched.

"More?"

Jen went to get more.

"What happened?" I asked Stacey. "How's Lindsey?"

"She's breathing on her own, but she's raving and none of us have any idea what she's talking about. Mike's recording her on his phone. How are you doing?"

"Chest hurts." I frowned as I took stock of myself. "And my leg and back."

She nodded. "You took a fall after you grabbed Lindsey's hand. Pretty quickly after that, you stopped breathing. I gave you mouth-to-mouth."

Jen returned with the water. I struggled upright. I was

laying on one of the chaise lounges from the patio. It had been dragged inside. I swung my feet over onto the floor and took the water, holding it carefully. My hands shook, and my head swam.

I drank the water about as fast as before.

"More?" Jen asked. Her expression was bland, but her eyes were turbulent.

"What happened?" Stacey asked, before I could respond.

"When I grabbed her hand, I got sucked into Lindsey's psychic space, and my body seemed to start behaving just like hers. Couldn't breath, couldn't let go. Only solution I could think of was Mitzi, so I summoned her binding stone, and she popped in. A lot too much like Aunty Mommy, if you ask me. I offered her a bargain. Took a little convincing, but she agreed to help Lindsey. Next thing I know, I'm looking up at you."

"What was the bargain?" Jen asked.

"Just that I was going to make an isolation box, so she could spend eternity with only herself for company and no outside stimulation whatsoever. If she helped Lindsey and agreed to teach her how to control her abilities, I'd let her continue in the world, still bound to the stone, of course."

"We were giving you CPR. What made you think you'd get out alive?" Stacey's question was almost nonchalant, like she hadn't been scared out of her mind, or furious at me for nearly dying and putting them through the emotional wringer.

I smirked. "Couldn't happen. You two weren't going to let me die. I knew that." Maybe my absolute certainty had been what convinced Mitzi. I looked around. Lindsey was in another chaise with Rhi and Lorel on either side, both trying to calm her. Her arms swung and her fingers wiggled in patterns that only she could see. She pantomimed writing. It seemed intricate, some of her gestures broad, others bare flicks of her fingers. The entire time she spoke. I couldn't understand a word. Several times a word or two sounded almost familiar, but it was all gobbledygook to me. Mikey stood at her feet with his phone held up, videoing her.

"Where's Luke?" I asked as I glanced around for Mitzi's rose quartz. "All of us women are accounted for. Did he find a hole in the fence?"

That got a small smile from both Stacey and Jen. I still couldn't tell if they were mad or not. I wouldn't apologize, though. I couldn't. I wouldn't have done anything differently.

"He's gone in search of some bandages and disinfectant. You cut your hand on that rock."

I glanced at my hand. A torn piece of cloth wrapped it. I pulled it aside and discovered Stacey was telling the truth, except the two wounds were more gouges than cuts. The side of the rock where it had broken off had sharp edges. I'd clutched it so hard I'd pressed wedged openings into my palm. Blood welled and started to fill my palm. I grimaced and closed my fist around the cloth to stem the bleeding.

"I guess if that's the worst of it, I'm coming out of this okay."

Jen snorted. "Some people would say that stopping breathing was the worst of it."

"Got any more water?" I asked, deciding that arguing would get me nowhere fast.

She gave me a disgusted look and disappeared behind the velvet curtain, returning a minute later with water, Luke trailing behind.

He carried a collection of things in his hands. His wary gaze fell on me.

"You okay?" He asked, crouching down in front of me and setting his supplies next to me on the chaise.

"Been worse."

He reached for my hand, taking away the torn cloth. He opened a brown bottle of hydrogen peroxide. "Might sting." He poured on my hand, using a hand towel underneath to catch the runoff. "Interesting night. This stuff happen to you a lot?"

"Just on days that end in -y."

"You told Mike you'd been protecting Stacey and Jen. From stuff like this?"

"Sometimes."

He dabbed my hand with another towel to dry it and started wrapping gauze around my palm.

"I'm beginning to see why Mike might be worried about what you bring to the table as far as Stacey's concerned."

"Fuck you, Luke," the woman in question said, hands on her hips. "I'll take twelve Becks over one of you, so you can shut your damned mouth and keep your idiotic opinions to yourself."

She shoved him aside and finished bandaging my hand, wrapping it in athletic tape to hold the gauze in place. She pushed my hand back onto my lap, then poked a sharp finger into my clavicle.

"Don't you go listening to Luke and Mike. I know how you are. You take your guilt trips very seriously, but we let you keep your secrets and let you wallow in your misplaced sense of responsibility for way too long. Not anymore. Jen, Lorraine, and I make our own choices, and nobody—not even you—gets to tell us who our friends are and what we do. Anything happens to us, that's on us. Got that?"

She'd kept stabbing me with her finger for the entire speech. I grabbed it in my healthy hand and held it away from me.

"Loud and clear. You can stop the woodpecker bit."

She glared and then snatched me in a tight hug. "I love you. You scared me."

I hugged her back and then Jen when she came in for a three-way.

"I wasn't scared," I said. "I knew you had me."

Jen scowled. "Scared the fuck out of me. I don't know CPR. Yet. I'm putting that on my to-do list ASAP. I'm not going to be that helpless again."

"I swear, if a genie ever pops out of a bottle for me, my first wish is going to be that you can only die after a long, healthy life," Stacey said. "All three of you."

"Same," Jen said. "Wait, if there are witches and psychics, does that mean there are genies too?"

I shrugged. "You've got me. I guess you'll have to start rubbing bottles to find out." I slid my loosely held fist back and forth to represent a man beating his meat.

That was enough to finally break the tension. All three of us broke into peals of laughter, while Luke stood watching.

We sobered quickly, remembering Lindsey. I stood and went to stand beside her, recapping to the others what had happened when I'd grabbed her hand.

"Her pulse is okay," Lorel said, knotting her fingers together. "So she's out of the woods as far as that goes. But how do we bring her back to herself? What's she doing?"

"Might want to get her a pen and some paper," Mikey suggested.

I glanced at him, wondering what he thought about all

of this. His expression remained cool and detached. He was in full cop-mode.

"She has something she's trying to capture," he continued. "She's repeating herself now. You might even want to let her have at a big wall or floor. Have a lot of pencils handy."

Watching her another minute, I agreed. "Where can we find a wall she can draw on? Something where she won't run out of space?"

"My place," Luke said. "I've got an indoor basketball court. Lots of wall space."

Lorel and Rhi exchanged a worried look.

"Might help her escape the vision if she can write it down," I said. "She might even be waiting to bring herself out until she can capture it."

"Okay," Rhi said with another look at Lorel, who nodded. "I drive an old VW Bug. It's too small to carry her like this."

"You can take my SUV," I said, pulling my keys out of my pocket. "The back seats fold down."

"What about you?" Lorel asked.

"I'll take your car. I can stop and get some markers to write with."

"*We'll* take your car," Stacey said, holding her hand out to Rhi for her keys. "I'll be driving."

"I'll drive these three to my house," Luke said, taking my keys. "Anybody else coming with me?"

"I'll ride with the three musketeers," Mikey said, pocketing his phone.

Jen rolled her eyes at me and mimed sticking her finger down her throat and throwing up. She glanced at Mikey. "You realize this isn't a date, right? Not only will you be the fourth wheel, you'll probably have to jam yourself in the back with me and ride with your knees up to your ears. You may want to rethink and go with Slutboy over here." She jerked her thumb at Luke.

The corner of his mouth kicked up. "Thanks for your concern, but I'll be fine."

"Actually, why doesn't Beck ride with us," Luke said. "I've got a bunch of extra bedrooms and you look like you're going to fall over at any moment."

I hesitated. As soon as he'd mentioned bedrooms, exhaustion had slammed into me like a Mack truck. My eyelids felt like twenty pound weights. I couldn't sleep, though. Not with Lindsey like this. I needed coffee. Gallons of it. I started shaking my head.

"Go," Stacey said. "Luke's right. We'll get what we need, and we'll all have a slumber party at Luke's." She glanced at Mikey. "Well, maybe not *all*."

"Oh, I wouldn't miss it for the world," he drawled.

"Just be sure to lock your door," Jen told me. "I'd hate for Luke to be incinerated because he decided to make a pass."

"I'd like to think I'd show restraint and just give him crabs or a serious case of male pattern baldness," I said.

"You might, but I'm not sure Damon would."

At the mention of his name, I felt a pang. He hadn't called or texted since he'd landed. Maybe distance didn't make the heart grow fonder. Maybe distance was all out of sight, out of mind.

I ignored the little throb of hurt kindled in my stomach. He'd had to go back for an emergency. By definition, those didn't leave leisure time. He loved me, and he missed me, and he'd call me when he could. Inwardly I rolled my eyes. Even though I knew that was true, I couldn't help the hollowness that opened in my chest, adding to the physical ache.

I had no idea why people wanted to be in love. It left you feeling uneasy and off-balance and lonely and stupid. Maybe Stacey was right not to get emotionally involved. Now, if I'd only realized that before I'd started having feelings for Damon, I'd be a whole lot better off.

"Will you pick up Ajax for me?" I asked Jen and Stacey, trying not to sound as forlorn as I suddenly felt. I'd left him at Lorraine's vet hospital. The staff spoiled him rotten and Lorraine would take him home after her surgery. He didn't like being separated from me, but given the night's original plan, he was better off with her.

"Of course," Stacey said. "Lorraine too."

"What do you call it when one guy cock blocks the other, but only so the target of their mutual affection can't get laid at all?" I asked Jen as Stacey, Mikey, and Luke left together to fetch the cars.

"Desperate?"

"I wonder how the boys see this ending."

"I figure it can go one of three ways: 1) menage a trois, 2) Stacey kills one or both, or 3)...." Jen trailed off, then shook her head. "Nope, there are only the two."

"You don't think Mikey will loosen up?"

She shrugged. "Doesn't seem the type. Luke's a lot more likely, but mouth-watering as he is, I don't know if Stacey could drink enough to take a ride on him. As far as she's concerned, he really is her brother. Deep down, I'm betting he agrees. He likes to flirt with her, but there's a line he's not going to cross. Come to think of it, that rules out a menage a trois, so the only way it can really go is murder. Only question is whether she'll kill both or just one, and if only one, which will be the first to drive her over the edge?"

"Luke," we both said together and then laughed.

By the time we got Lindsey loaded in the Highlander, I could barely keep my eyes open. I did manage to remember to retrieve Mitzi's quartz prison. My blood still smeared it. I was happy to find our psychic connection hadn't continued. Or maybe she just wasn't talking to me. If so, she'd be unhappy to learn that suited me down to the ground. With a sigh, I shoved her in my pocket. I owed her some sightseeing, and Lindsey might need her. Maybe I ought to leave her on Luke's nightstand. She'd certainly get an eyeful.

That thought made me smile all the way to the car until I fell asleep.

# CHAPTER SEVEN

I woke to the sounds of arguing. I stretched and yawned, looking down at Ajax, who sprawled across my legs. I scratched his ears, and he made a happy sound, and promptly wriggled himself around so I could scratch his tummy.

"What's going on, boy?" I asked with a smile.

The previous night—actually morning—I'd zombied into one of Luke's guest bedrooms. I'd found a stock of unused toiletries and proceeded to brush my teeth before stripping down to my underwear and crawling straight into bed. I hadn't even stirred when Ajax joined me.

The argument grew louder. I recognized Stacey's voice and Luke's lower rumble. Sibling spat? I couldn't hear what the fight was about, but I knew I wouldn't be going back to sleep anytime soon.

I dragged myself out of bed, much to Ajax's annoyance, and went to grab a shower. My chest hurt like fuck. I probably had a broken rib or two.

I found a canvas bag containing a pair of jeans, fresh underwear, a tee shirt, and socks in the sink. Stacey and Jen must have stopped at the hotel and raided my closet. Now if they'd only brought an IV of coffee and a bunch of ibuprofen, I'd be set.

I rifled through the medicine cabinet and found an unopened bottle. I palmed four and swallowed them dry.

After I'd showered and dressed, I headed downstairs. Hopefully Luke had food Ajax could eat.

Luke's house was built in the Frank Lloyd Wright style. It nested into the hillside and surrounding oaks. Despite its size—easily ten thousand square feet—It felt cozy and warm with a lot of windows, wood floors, and mid-century modern furnishings. Luke didn't go for chrome and steel or black and white, thank goodness. The modern look was chic, but I found it incredibly boring.

The argument had become a rumble of conversation. I wandered through several big rooms intended for entertaining crowds, pausing here and there to examine the artwork and furniture. Sunshine fell through the tall windows and splashed across the comfortable couches and chairs. I checked my phone for the time. Ten o'clock. I hadn't planned to sleep so late.

Eventually I meandered my way to the kitchen. It was a chef's wet dream. It had high end appliances, a six-burner stove with a griddle and a grill, a walk in refrigerator and freezer, a giant wine fridge, a vast pantry, an island that went on for days, a chunky oak table that sat twenty, plus every other bell and whistle a chef might want.

I wiped my chin to make sure I hadn't drooled. To get a chance to cook in this kitchen, I'd have considered going down on Luke. Of course Damon would point out that I had plenty of money to create a kitchen at least this fancy. He'd also go caveman on me. What that would entail I wasn't sure, but it wouldn't be pretty, and poor Luke would probably come out of it with broken bones.

I turned my attention to the tableau before me. Mikey, Stacey, and Jen sat on one side of the island. Luke leaned against the far counter, his arms crossed and looking defensive.

"I get tons of invitations," he was telling Stacey, who looked furious. "Most of them are from people I don't even know. They want me to go to this gala or this fundraiser or who even knows. Most of the time I don't even open them."

"You opened this one," she shot back.

"Because I know he's a social-climbing slime-bucket."

She shook her head and tossed up her hands. "How does that even make sense? You open the invite *because* you don't like him?"

"Maybe Luke's from Earth 2," I suggested with another yawn, while holding up two fingers. "I hear things don't actually have to make sense there." My gaze riveted on the espresso machine peeking out from behind him.

"Get out of the way, Luke," Jen said. "You never want to stand between Beck and her coffee. You might lose your favorite appendage."

Stacey shooed him aside. "I'll fix it, Beck. Get some sugar, Luke. Hurry, before she goes feral."

I'd have protested, but they weren't wrong about me. My blood was at least three quarters coffee.

"What's going on?" I asked. My stomach growled. I headed for the refrigerator and started digging out ingredients for an omelet. I found some ground turkey. Perfect for Ajax. I carried my bounty to the island, where the stove sat at one end. I quickly fired up the grill, made patties from the turkey, and tossed them on the heat. I then set about chopping veggies.

"Luke has an invitation to that garden party. You know, the one being held by Lydia's asshole ex? The same guy who stole her cats, had her arrested, got her fired from several jobs, and had her evicted from her apartment."

Stacey gave Luke a baleful look, the espresso machine starting to steam loudly. "I knew you kept crap company, but I never thought you'd be caught dead around a rattlesnake like him."

He closed his eyes and tipped his head back, letting out a gusty sigh. "I will say it again. I don't know the man. He's got political ambitions, and I'm on a dozen lists he could buy to solicit donations."

"Which you opened," she pointed out. "Even though you don't usually."

"Have a look at the address. The return address," he clarified when she picked up the envelope.

She frowned. "This is right up the road."

He nodded. "The Robinsons used to live there. Nice people. I didn't know the property changed hands, or that that asshole had bought it. I opened the invite because I was curious about what he's up to. He's looking for money to fund a run for the state senate."

"You didn't RSVP," she said, turning the reply card in her fingers thoughtfully.

"Where's Lorraine?" I asked, moving on to dicing potatoes after flipping the turkey burgers.

Stacey set the card down and brought my coffee over, which was actually six or eight shots of espresso with steamed milk and plenty of sugar. I sipped. Liquid bliss.

"She'll be back soon. She went to check on the horse she operated on last night."

"It went okay?"

"Lorraine was pretty confident the mare would be fine," Jen said.

"Anybody hungry?" I asked, as I rifled the cupboards for oil and spices. I tossed a mixture of potatoes, bell peppers, and onions with olive oil and a variety of spices, then poured them on a giant jelly roll sheet and slid them into the oven.

Up to this point, Officer Mikey had remained quiet, but he added his voice to the chorus of affirmatives.

"How are you feeling?" he asked.

I had to admit I looked at him like his hair was on fire. Of all the people to ask me that question, I'd have put him at the bottom of the list. Crossed off in thick black Sharpie.

"Good. Sore, but the shower helped." In fact, I had bruises on my chest, hip, knee, and side, but he didn't need to hear about those. "Where are Lindsey and her cousins?"

"Asleep," Luke said. "When we got her into the gym she went nuts. I mean demented. Frantic. Like she was hopped up on a truckload of meth. She went to town on the walls. Pens I gave her ran out of ink in nothing flat."

"We got here just in time with supplies," Jen added, sipping on her orange juice. "Luke's right. She was in a frenzy. Focused and manic. She wrote on the walls and the floor, and it was nothing any of us could understand. Diagrams and words that weren't words. At least they weren't English."

"As soon as she was done, she collapsed," Stacey said. "She was soaked with sweat, and she'd broken another blood vessel. Her eyes looked like they were bleeding. I'm not sure, but she looked like she might have lost twenty pounds. Her clothes hung on her. Rhi and Lorel had been trying to get her to eat and drink, but she couldn't or wouldn't stop or slow down."

Curiosity gnawed at me, but breakfast demanded I stay and eat before wandering off to look at the results of Lindsey's fugue.

"Grate some Parmesan, would you?" I asked Luke. "And some Gruyere. Mikey, make yourself useful and stir the potatoes."

Both stood and went to work.

"Anything we can do?" Jen asked.

"Drinks, set the table, make toast. Oh, crap!"

"What?"

"I'm supposed to meet my mother for lunch today. I need to text her." I pulled out my cell and tapped out the message, saying an emergency had come up, but we could reschedule for tomorrow if she had time. I sent it and went back to cooking.

"We should use the invitation," Stacey announced, while buttering a batch of rye toast.

"You planning to start a fire?" Luke asked. "I know I haven't run out of toilet paper, so you can't be wanting to use it for that."

She made a face at him. "Don't be an idiot. I mean we could go to the party and get Lydia's cats."

"Whose cats?"

"Lydia. Carson Flannery, the asshole up the road, is her ex, and he's been terrorizing her." She went on to explain the whole story, finishing up with, "so we're going to take the cats back and make him stop harassing her."

"You're talking about theft," Mikey said with a frown. "You could get arrested. And how would you make him do anything?"

"I've got a few ideas."

"Do tell."

She shook her head. "The only reason you're involved in

this at all is because I want Lydia to have a solid alibi. I was going to have you hang out with her after her shift last night while we did what we needed to do."

"You thought I'd just go along with this idiocy, knowing you're off to commit who knows what crimes?"

Mikey's voice went so cold I could almost see the icicles hanging off his words. Stacey was unfazed.

"I hoped," she said. "But just in case you wouldn't, I called Luke as a back-up. Flannery has a lot of connections, and I thought an alibi from an officer of the law would be best, but Luke's rich and well-connected, so he'll do."

Officer Mikey actually growled at that revelation.

"It's not like you want to do it, so I don't know what your damage is," she said tartly.

"*You* need to keep your hands to yourself," she said, turning to Luke. "Lydia's fragile right now. She's been through hell, and if her ex has his way, he'll drag her back to his home and lock her in a basement or something. I'm not letting that happen."

"*We're* not going to let that happen," Lorraine corrected as she stepped into the kitchen.

She was dressed in a flowing sleeveless jumpsuit, patterned with brilliant yellow hibiscus flowers on a cobalt background. Her thick chestnut hair fell in waves over her shoulders, her dramatic smokey black and blue eyeshadow and ruby lips making her look mysterious and exotic. She wore her nails short and her hands were callused. When she wasn't working with her animals, she was digging in her garden. If Jen was an Amazon and Stacey a pixie, Lorraine was mother earth.

She tossed her handbag on the counter and went to make herself espresso. She looked over her shoulder at me. "Refill?"

I grinned. "Always. You want breakfast?"

She flashed a smile of her own. "Always."

"What exactly do you expect me to do while you go and commit whatever crimes you have in mind?" Mikey asked, his expression turning to granite.

"Nothing," Stacey said dismissively. "Go home and mow the lawn, or whatever you do on a Sunday."

His lip curled, and he gave a slow shake of his head. "Are you serious or just trying to piss me off?"

She put her hands on her hips, her eyes sparking with irritation. "You want me to apologize for wasting your time? Or for getting you involved at all? You got it. I'm sorry. I should have known better. You're too straight an arrow to help with this." She made the last sound like an insult.

"I don't know why I thought you'd be different from the police idiots who have all taken Flannery's word for everything. They won't even listen to Lydia. She's just the bitter ex-wife causing the poor, pitiful man trouble." She glared at Mikey, clearly counting him among the cops who chose to ignore Lydia's plight. "*I'm* the only one who listened. Since neither you nor your cop buddies will do anything, we're going to get her cats back, and we're going to make sure Flannery stops bothering her. Besides, is it really theft if we steal back what he stole?"

"I can't be Lydia's alibi," Luke said, as if she hadn't just ripped Mikey a new asshole. "The invitation is to me, so I'll have to go to the party. Beck would be my obvious date. She's got the name recognition of her aunt, and everybody will expect that she's inherited a bunch of money. That makes her welcome, and Flannery will be eager to suck up to us both."

"What do we do about Lydia?" Jen asked. "And how do the rest of us get into the party?"

"You're the best choice to give Lydia her alibi, Stacey," I said with an apologetic look. I knew how much she wanted to be the one to teach the asshole ex a lesson or at least be there to witness it. "You're the only one of us who actually knows her, and it makes sense that you would go do something together. When the cops question her—and given their track record so far, they will—they won't wonder why she was with strangers. Wouldn't hurt if you had an alibi either."

Her lips flattened and her eyes narrowed. She crossed her arms, her chin jutting. I just waited. I knew she'd be mad, but she wasn't stupid. A minute ticked by, and I worked at cracking eggs into a bowl.

"Fine," she spat out finally. "I'll call her, but you remember this moment, Beck, when I use logic against *you*." Her finger stabbed the air as she pointed at me.

"I'll try," I said, as she spun around and marched out of the room, digging in her pocket for her phone as she went.

"That takes care of Lydia, but what about me and Lorraine?" Jen asked. "You aren't going to be able to get the cats if you and Luke are at the party. We need to get in under the radar."

"Like as caterers or something," Lorraine said, sitting next to Jen and casting a wary look at Mikey.

"I'll cast a glamour," I said, not looking up.

"What does that mean?" Luke asked, and he'd clearly not quite come to terms with magic, because his voice cracked like he'd just hit puberty.

"A disguise, right?" Jen said.

"Sort of, but in this case, I'd make it so nobody wants to notice you. They'll see you, but they won't pay any attention. You'll be able to walk in with me and Luke."

Jen grinned and Lorraine's eyes rounded. "You can do that?" she asked.

I nodded and reached for the whisk. "As long as you don't do something that seriously calls attention to yourself, for all practical purposes, you'll be invisible."

"What do you mean by 'seriously calls attention to ourselves'?" Lorraine asked, tapping her fingers on the counter.

"And what happens if we do?" Jen added.

"The glamour essentially convinces people not to pay any attention to you. They might look straight at you but won't be able to remember seeing you, or if they do, they won't be able to remember anything about what you look like. That said, you can break the glamour by essentially forcing them to see you."

"Like what would do it?" Jen asked.

I shrugged. "Stripping naked could do it, but screaming and throwing dishes definitely would. Everybody's got a different threshold, though, so it's best to be as unassuming as possible."

"Oh, goody. We're such experts at fading into the background," Jen said. "We may be doomed."

"You'll just have to work hard," I told her. The four of us had a habit of stealing the spotlight. Not that we meant to, but for some reason, when you didn't give a lot of fucks about what people think of you, they tend to give you more attention.

"Would walking out with the cats constitute calling attention to themselves?" Mikey inserted suddenly.

I lifted a brow at him and resumed beating the eggs. "Could. Depends on how unexpected or out of place they seem, but that's where I come in. I'll create a distraction."

"What kind of distraction?" He scowled, no doubt

imagining me burning down the house or maybe calling down a meteor strike. If only.

I shrugged. "A swarm of bees? Cockroaches? A small tornado? I have no idea. It all depends on the situation. Hell, I could let Mitzi loose. I bet she'd love to go full-on poltergeist again."

Just at the moment, she was in my pocket, no doubt listening to every word.

I set the eggs aside and turned on two burners, generously adding butter to two pans. I divided the vegetables between them and gave them a quick sauté.

"Okay, she and I are going to spend the day shopping and maybe see a movie and have dinner," Stacey announced as she returned. She sat on the other side of Jen and looked across at Mikey. "What are you still doing here?"

"I'm hungry."

"There are other places to eat."

"I like it here."

"I didn't realize you were into sadomasochism. I thought you were strictly vanilla," she taunted.

"You don't have a clue what I am," he shot back.

"Right back at ya, Slick," she snapped and stood up. "And that is my cue to step off. I'll take a raincheck on the eggs. Let me know how the party goes. Luke, can I borrow your car?"

"Stacey," Mikey began, but she'd stalked out of the room.

Luke followed. Mikey stood as if he intended to do the same, but Lorraine stopped him.

"If you don't want her to rip your dick off, you should probably stay here."

"I'm not going to just let her walk out. We're going to

settle this now." He was seething, the cold having turned volcanic.

"How exactly do you see that going?" Jen asked, tipping her head to the side.

"I don't know, but it's time we had it out."

"Definitely," Lorraine said. "Go do that. It was somewhat nice knowing you. Don't let the door hit you in the ass on the way out."

He went a couple more steps and stopped, turning to look at her. "What do you suggest I do?"

"Pull your head out of your ass, for one," she said. "Stop being so goddamned judgmental. For a guy who claims to like her, you sure treat her like something you stepped in."

"If it's true she has no idea who you are, ask yourself why," Jen added. "Whose fault is that?"

"A relationship takes two," he huffed.

I couldn't keep my mouth shut any longer. "You know, you're so busy handing out rules for how Stacey should act that you don't realize how condescending and rude your demands are. She's a grown-ass woman who doesn't need to twist herself into a new shape just so you'll approve of her. Or is it more that you won't be disgusted at yourself for wanting her? Turn her into Stepford Stacey, so you don't mind being seen in public with her? Why would she ever participate in a relationship with a man who treats her like that? I sure as hell wouldn't."

I set aside the vegetables, tossed more butter in the pans, and ladled in the eggs, not bothering to look at Mikey to see how he reacted to my words. I turned the heat down and went to check the potatoes as Luke returned.

"She left," he said, sauntering over to make himself another espresso. "Hopefully she doesn't drive so pissed she wraps the car around a tree."

"Not likely," I said.

"She was pretty hot." He looked at Mikey. "Keep that up, would you? Every time you poke pins in her, she gets closer to my bed."

"You wish," Lorraine said.

"I'll only make her feel good," he said. "I'm a safe space. That jackass—" He pointed at Mikey. "—spends all his time trying to make her feel small and unworthy. I just want to celebrate her."

"Her body, you mean," Jen said with an eyeroll.

"Sure. I love her body, but I love the rest of her, too." He leveled a stoney look at Mikey. "I love her just the way she is."

Lorraine, Jen, and I exchanged a startled glance. Love? Did he mean that? Or was it a figure of speech? And if he did mean it, what sort of love? The kind he had for a favorite pair of shoes or piece of art? Or the real kind?

"Maybe you should leave, too," Luke told Mikey. "You don't want to be involved. If you stay, you will be."

The other man stiffened and nodded. "I'll call a cab." With that, he walked out.

"And then there were four," Lorraine said, sipping from her cup. "How are we going to do this cat burglary?"

I finished with the omelets, and we ate, discussing our options. We had no idea where the cats were, or if they were even on the property.

"Is there any magic you can do to find out?" Luke asked me.

"I've never been able to locate things or people," I said. "I'm sure there must be a way, but if there is, I don't know it."

"Then we just have to search. When you think about it, he probably isn't hiding them. As far as he knows, the only person who might come after them is Lydia, and there's no way she's getting in without him or his security finding out," Lorraine said.

"You make it sound like he's using them for bait," Jen said, cocking her head thoughtfully.

"He could be. Think about it. He's harassing her, stalking her, stealing from her, reporting her to the police for things she didn't do, getting her evicted, and making her lose her jobs, but all of those only isolate her and make her desperate. If she gets desperate enough, he can swoop in and get her under his control again," Lorraine said.

"It's definitely a possibility. Stacey didn't say why she left him, or if he wanted her to go. Maybe all of this really is a ploy to lure her back. Or force her back." I frowned. "But why would he want to have a wife who hates and fears him if he's running for office? Wouldn't she be a liability?"

"She's made accusations against him, even if no one believes them," Luke said. "His opponent would use those to attack his campaign. The accusations become a lot less compelling if Lydia goes back to his bed and even recants and says she was just angry and wanted to hurt him or some bullshit," Luke said. "If that's his goal, he hasn't got a lot of time. Not if this party is kicking off his fundraising. He'll have to declare he's running soon, and he needs her toeing line by then."

"Is it me, or is anybody else worried about what he might do to the cats?" Lorraine asked, setting her fork down, her face growing pale.

"How do you mean?" I asked, but I was already putting the pieces together, and they weren't pretty.

"What if he's holding them hostage? I know a lot of people wouldn't sacrifice a lot for their pets, but a lot of people would." She looked at me. "What wouldn't you do for Ajax?"

"I'd burn the city down," I said without hesitation. It sounded like hyperbole, and maybe I wouldn't actually burn the city, but I'd risk my life to save his. I knew that without a doubt.

"These cats are all that Lydia has left. Flannery would know what they mean to her. So maybe he steals them and tells her if she doesn't come back and tell the world she's been an awful wife and lied, that now she wants to be the wife he deserves and blah blah blah, then he'll kill them. Hell, he might convince her he's serious by maiming one, or even killing it."

All three of us stared at her. My mouth went dry, and I reached down to pet Ajax. He'd come to lay just behind my chair. He caught my mood and sat, resting his head on my lap, his liquid gaze full of love and trust.

As far as I was concerned, Aunty Mommy had been the most evil person I knew or could imagine, but this sort of thing was next level cruel. Animals were innocent and loved unconditionally. They deserved everything wonderful in life. I'd rescued Ajax from a horrific situation where he'd been kept on a short chain, his collar chewing into his neck, his skin covered in sores. He'd been starved and scared and angry, and he'd been protecting two little girls from their homicidal father. I'd been glad when the bastard was killed. The fucker deserved it. He deserved a lot worse, and I hoped he was getting his full due in hell. But that had been casual neglect, which was awful enough. What Lorraine was talking about now was sadistic. Evil.

"That's..." I didn't even have the words.

Jen nodded. "That's fucked up, insane, and hopefully way outside of reality."

"Trouble is, it makes a lot of sense," Luke said.

"Only if Flannery is a psychopath," I said, hoping like fuck that he wasn't.

"He's a politician. Aren't they psychopaths by definition?" Lorraine asked. "Everything for them is about power, money, and getting more of both."

Her cynicism was well earned. Her own father had abandoned his family when she was young and had gone on to have a celebrated career, first as a federal judge, then as a senator. Years ago he'd guaranteed that success by forcing her mother to sign a non-disclosure agreement, saying she wouldn't ever reveal he'd fathered Lorraine or that he'd abandoned her, and in exchange he'd give her a substantial payoff and would pay for Lorraine's college and vet school, and he'd smooth the way in her career in any way she needed. She'd have to repay all the money if she or Lorraine ever revealed the truth. He'd gone so far as to have himself removed from her birth certificate, though how he'd done that, I had no idea. It hadn't been legal, that's for sure. He'd had their marriage nullified as well.

He was now jockeying to either get on the Supreme Court, or become the Attorney General of the United States.

Like Lorraine said: psychopath.

"Whatever his plans, he won't risk doing anything during his party," I said. "We'll just have to make sure he can't do anything after." I picked up the invitation and glanced at the clock. "It's already started."

"We've got time." Luke said, taking it from me. "The party will go on until late, no doubt with rivers of alcohol to loosen up the checkbooks. Most people will be fashionably late, anyhow."

"One problem," I said. "I don't have anything to wear. I lost my wardrobe when Garrett destroyed my apartment.

I'll have to see if I can find anything off the rack somewhere."

"Or..." Jen said, drawing the word out.

I eyed her, sure I was going to hate her next words. I was so right.

"You could raid Aunty Mommy's closet."

"No," my mouth said before my brain even got a chance to think about it.

"You're close enough to her size to find something, and you could probably wiggle your nose and make both the clothes and shoes fit."

"I'd rather go naked."

"That would certainly distract Flannery," Lorraine said.

"It would also get you tossed out," Jen said. She glared at Luke. "And keep your mouth shut. We already know you'd support her going naked." She turned back to me. "Up to you, but you know you're more likely to find something at Aunty Mommy's than at some store. You're stuck with whatever's open on Sunday, which is going to be the mall and Walmart."

I glared. I hated that she was right. I wasn't going to say it out loud, either.

"We might be able to help."

Rhi stood in the door. Her eyes were bruised looking and tired. I jumped up.

"How are you? How's Lindsey? Are you hungry? Sit down."

I ushered her to my now-empty chair, scooped up my dishes and went to make her an omelet. Ajax followed, leaning against my leg. Talk about an emotional support animal. I was supposed to be his support.

"Lindsey's still asleep. Lorel is staying with her."

"I'll fix her something to eat and take it to her."

"What did you mean you might be able to help?" Lorraine asked after I introduced her.

"Lorel and I design clothes. A lot of A-listers wear them. In fact, we've designed for Lydia Flannery. She's lovely, and her husband is scum. I'd love to help her. I know we have something you could wear. We'd just have to run to our house in Sutton."

She hesitated, looking around at all of us and flushing when she met Luke's admiring gaze and quickly looking away. I rolled my eyes. He was such a tomcat.

"You're looking for something special, aren't you?" She sounded uncertain.

"For a garden party," I explained. "I need to look rich and eager to give away my money to a hungry politician."

"I have some things that would definitely work," she said.

I slid the omelet onto the plate and sprinkled some Gruyere and Parmesan on top, and added some of the potatoes I'd left in the warming oven. I put it down in front of her and pushed the plate of toast in her direction.

"What would you like to drink?"

"Tea would be good. If you have any."

"Luke?"

"Pantry, left side, third shelf."

I opened the door. "Got a favorite?" I called to Rhi.

"Earl Gray or Orange Pekoe."

I grabbed both, along with a handy diffuser and set them on the table before grabbing a cup and drawing hot water from the spigot on the espresso machine.

"Cream or sugar?"

"No, thank you."

I set the hot water down and went to get Lorel's plate ready.

"Should I make something for Lindsey?" I asked. "Do you think she'll wake up soon?"

A shrug. "I wish I knew. I've never seen a vision take her like this. Did you see what she did?"

I shook my head. "I didn't."

"You need to. Whatever it is, it's for you."

"For me?"

Rhi nodded. "She said you were going to need it. She said…"

"What?"

She looked down and took a breath and looked back at me. "She said you're running out of time."

My brows stitched together. "Running out of time for what?"

She shook her head. "I'm sorry. I don't know. I'm hoping she'll be able to say more when she wakes up, but she usually doesn't remember anything.

I grimaced. "That's helpful."

"At least you're forewarned. That's good, right?"

"Only if the shit doesn't hit the fan first." Since my stars always aligned under the influence of Murphy's Law, the shit storm was inevitable. The only real question, how bad would it be? My stomach curled with foreboding and I shuddered as a shadow wrapped around me.

Whatever disaster was coming for me, it promised to be very bad indeed.

# CHAPTER EIGHT

"So now we mingle," Luke said, his hand touching bare skin at the center of my back.

We'd arrived at Carson Flannery's garden party closer to five than four. I was dressed in an elegant green dress. It wrapped my neck and left my shoulders and back bare all the way down to just above the curve of my ass. A sexy weaving of thin strips of fabric played peek-a-boo with onlookers, while keeping the back from gaping open. Made of silk charmeuse, it flowed over my body to a couple inches above my knees, giving it a semi-conservative appearance, instantly belied by the slit running up to the top of my thigh. Rhi had finished it off with a pair of stiletto pumps, the heel made of clear acrylic, the rest constructed of emerald cloth and mesh to match the dress.

I don't know that I'd ever looked so good. Luke's eyes had almost bugged out of his head when he saw me, which only made me sad that he wasn't Damon. When he rested his hand in the small of my back, I didn't get even the slightest jolt of electricity. With Damon, I'd have been buzzing like a live wire. I set that aside to consider later.

He still hadn't called or even texted since the one telling me he'd landed. That should have irritated me, but the business with Lindsey made me worry instead. Her warning was so vague—something bad was coming. That could mean almost anything. Her frenetic activities last night had only increased my uneasiness.

I was starting to feel like I was standing blindfolded on the railroad tracks, and it was only a matter of time before a train mowed me down. My skin itched with a constant warning, but I had no idea what to do. How did I protect myself from an unknown problem so vaguely defined as... something bad?

"Beck?"

Luke's voice called me back to the present. We were walking along a stone path, the afternoon sun gleaming through the canopy of leaves shading us.

"What?"

"Are you alright?"

"Just wondering how Lorraine and Jen are doing." My phone gave off a scroll of musical notes. Stacey. I pulled the cell out of my clutch and answered.

"What's up?"

"Lydia's gone."

"Gone?" I echoed, the foreboding in my stomach twisting tighter. "Where? When?"

"We went shopping and stopped to eat. She got a call and went outside. She never came back. I went to look for her and her car was gone."

"Where are you?"

"I called an Uber. I'm on my way to the party."

I nodded. "I'll have Luke meet you and escort you inside."

"I've got a bad feeling about this, Beck. She wouldn't

have just left without telling me. She must have had a good reason."

"You mean Flannery."

"I don't know. I didn't tell her you were going after the cats at all, much less today. I wanted her to be totally surprised if and when the cops questioned her." The worry in her voice was palpable. "What if Flannery threatened to hurt the kitties unless she came to see him? By making her take her car, he could claim she came of her own free will."

"We're here at the party. I'll look for her."

"What if he had someone kidnap her? She could be anywhere." Stacey's voice pinched off like she was trying not to panic.

"We'll find her. Let Luke know when you get here."

After I hung up, I explained the situation to Luke, while texting Jen and Lorraine to keep their eyes open. My glamour had worked exactly as I'd planned. Luke and I had been stopped by security to check our invitation, and Jen and Lorraine had walked in on our heels with no questions asked. They might as well have been invisible.

Once inside, they'd gone in search of the cats, and we'd headed for the pavilion, which was really just an oversized gazebo. Really oversized. A band played off to the side of the central dance floor. On the other side was one of several bars. Seating areas had been situated in shady spots. Water ran along a carefully constructed course, tinkling over small waterfalls and flowing into a fish pond and then out to wind through the vast yard. Flowers bloomed, battling with the scents of food.

The catering was set up on a patio, with tables scattered over the lawn. Clusters of people stood about chatting, and a few danced.

"I hate these things," Luke said softly as he collected a

glass of white wine and a scotch and water from the bar. He handed me the wine glass. "What do you want to do now?"

"Meet Flannery." I couldn't help smiling. It wasn't friendly. I had a plan for Flannery, but to implement it, I needed to touch him. I hadn't told anybody else my plan, but the asshole had a lifetime of unexpected misery coming.

"He's over there." Luke motioned with his chin. "Talking to Gloria Machado."

"I know her. I've sold her some furniture and jewelry before." I started across the lawn.

Gloria was a force of nature. Somewhere in her seventies, she was vigorous, outspoken, and didn't take crap from anybody. She dyed her hair scarlet and wore masculine clothing, usually with a vest and tie. She came from one of the oldest families in the state and had money to burn. Seeing her here didn't surprise me at all.

As I drew closer, I examined Carson Flannery. I guessed he was in his mid-thirties. He had the look of someone who cared a lot for their appearance. It never hurt to be good looking when running for office.

He wore gray pants and jacket, a white shirt, and wingtips. His hair was a light brown and had enough product in it to protect it from a hurricane. He had a casual Cary Grant air about him. It made him seem debonair and world-wise, while at the same time, he seemed entranced by everything Gloria said.

His appearance didn't match up with the stories of what he'd done to Lydia, but abusers had a knack for disguises. An ambitious man like him would hide all his viciousness and ruthlessness behind a genial mask, while doing whatever necessary to climb the political ladder, making all the money he could along the way.

He looked up as we approached, and I saw a flicker of annoyance cross his face, no doubt because we were interrupting his sales pitch with Gloria. That meant he didn't recognize Luke or me. Since I hadn't been invited, not knowing me made sense, but Luke was his neighbor and equaled Gloria in wealth. Thanks to Aunty Mommy, I probably had more money than both of them put together, but I'd just as soon not advertise that fact. Not that I had a choice. My guess was he had handlers in his ear telling him everything he needed to know about whoever he was talking to, so he could appear suave and knowledgeable and therefore a good candidate for state senate. He'd probably have our shoe sizes within a minute.

Gloria followed his gaze and smiled widely at me.

"Beck! It's delightful to see you." She wrapped me in a hug and stood back, surveying me. "You look amazing. That dress! Turn around and let me see you."

She spoke rapid-fire, and I humored her, turning in a circle.

"Exquisite! Who are you wearing?"

"Her name is Rhiannon Larson. She's new to me, but I couldn't say no to this dress." I smoothed my hand over the fabric.

"Nor should you," Gloria said. "I'll want her contact information. And who is your charming companion?" She cast an admiring look over Luke, who'd dressed like a cruise ship captain in white slacks and a navy jacket.

Everything fit him like it was made for him, which of course it was. He was the picture of effortless chic, like he'd thrown on whatever was at hand and managed to look like he'd spent hours getting dressed. I was sure Flannery had spent far longer on his preparations.

"This is Luke Conley. Luke, this is Gloria Machado."

He took Gloria's proffered hand and held it between his, looking at her like she was the only woman on the planet. "Delighted, Gloria. I couldn't be more pleased to meet you."

I wanted to roll my eyes at the subtle emphasis on the last word, but he had his part down and played it to the hilt. Gloria smiled, delighted.

"Hello and welcome," Flannery said, chiseling into the conversation with an ingratiating smile. He held his hand out to Luke. "I'm Carson Flannery. Glad you could make it. Thanks for coming."

Luke glanced at the other man's hand, his brows arching, and slowly let go of Gloria. He hesitated another moment before taking Flannery's hand. That momentary pause and the disdain of his eyebrows made Flannery's lips tighten, and me marvel at Luke's skill in playing the social game.

"Of course. I'm pleased to make your acquaintance," Luke replied, giving a short, fast shake before pulling away. "This is Beck Wyatt."

He didn't explain who I was, but Gloria's interaction with me said I was Someone. As in, I might have money, connections, or the ability to find him donors.

His smile turned sickly sweet, and he took my hand, holding it for too long, like a man who was used to having women fall into his bed. His gaze swept over me and back up, no doubt meaning to be complementary and totally making me want to throw up on his shoes.

"I'm pleased you could come to my little gathering. I'd love to show you around, if I may."

I restrained myself from telling him to fuck off. The man was sure he was handsome and charming and everything a woman could want. His confidence bordered on arrogance. On Luke, that attitude was somehow charming. Flannery was just repulsive. I wouldn't have minded popping his ego, but I was on a mission, and I couldn't indulge my irritation. I smiled as if I was falling for his charm.

"That would be lovely. Gloria, would you like to join us?"

The other woman fluttered her fingers dismissively. "No, no. You go ahead. I want to go say hello to some friends."

Luke put a possessive hand on my back. "I guess it's just us, then."

He smiled and winked at me, the humor not reaching his eyes. He didn't like Flannery any more than I did. The man was slimy and smarmy. Exactly the sort of person nobody needed in public service.

It was clear he had a singular agenda, talking about what he'd like to accomplish for the state and how humble he was and eager to earn our support. I mostly tuned him out, letting Luke suffer Flannery's tedious overtures.

"Are you married, Mr. Flannery?" I asked suddenly, when his talk about the importance of family and marriage percolated through my disinterest.

He gave an artfully abashed look. "I'm afraid I haven't been lucky in love."

No doubt he figured that I'd take that as an answer. No such luck.

I smiled blandly. "I'm sorry for being obtuse, but does that mean you are married? Or maybe divorced?"

He hesitated, clearly trying to sort out the answer. I bumbled on.

"Marriage is so important for the people who are in office, don't you think? Otherwise how will they know what ordinary people go through, especially raising children? I don't think I could support someone who hadn't experienced what so many of his constituents go through every day." I looked at Luke. "Don't you think so, Baby?"

The last was way over the top, and both Luke and I knew it. I could see him trying to fight off laughter. I blinked my eyelashes. He slipped his arm around my back and pulled me close, his hand caressing my hip.

"Absolutely, Sweetheart," he said, dropping a kiss on my cheek before looking back at Flannery. "I would have guessed you're married, since you bought this place. It's a perfect family home."

"I'm afraid my situation is a little complicated," Flannery said. "My wife and I have been estranged, but we've been working with a counselor, and I think we'll be back together very soon. She's got some... problems... you see, and she didn't want to hurt my career, so she left. I'm doing all I can to convince her to come home. I love her so much."

He actually managed to look teary at that confession. He cleared his throat and offered an unsteady smile. "I'm sorry. I hope you don't mind if I excuse myself. I need to speak to my other guests."

"Of course," Luke said. "Maybe we can talk soon about your thoughts on Proposition ninety-eight."

Relief swept Flannery's face. "I would be happy to. Maybe we can set up a meeting next week?"

"I'll have to check my calendar, but I'm sure I could figure something out," Luke said.

"My secretary will call you. Please excuse me."

We watched Flannery walk away. His phone rang and he answered. A moment later he hung up and hurried in the direction of the house.

"He hopes he'll be back together with his wife soon? Does that mean he and Lydia aren't divorced yet?" I asked.

"Sounds like it, and it sounds like he's got a story ready for the press when he forces her back home."

"Why wouldn't he just let her go? Pay her off, so she doesn't sabotage his career? He can't possibly love her, so why is he so determined to pull her back?"

"Some men can't stand getting left behind. Especially when they think they own their spouse," Luke said. "She's property, and property does what it's told. He can't stand the idea that she'd leave him, and he couldn't stop her. He needs to control her and force her to do whatever he says. He wants to see her cave in to him every day in every way. If he was abusive before—and it's a safe bet he was—it'll only get worse if he gets her back. He'll tell her she can leave any time, but she'll know she can't. He'll have shown her he can do anything he wants to her, and no one will stop him. If I had to guess, I'd say he'll get her to do something illegal or embarrassing and blackmail her with it for the rest of her life."

I could imagine what he might make her do, and I probably wasn't nearly depraved enough to come up with all the possibilities Flannery would.

"What are you going to do to him?" Luke asked. "Or did you already do it?"

I'd meant to curse him as soon as I saw him, but I'd let myself get distracted. I needed to touch him, but I didn't want to take the time to corner him.

"Let's go help look for Lydia and the cats," I said, turning toward the house.

The place was bigger than Luke's, and instead of the mid-century modern look of Frank Lloyd Wright, it was all French chateau. Where Luke's house tried to be one with the landscape, Flannery's stood out like it wanted to make a statement. It was made of stone and brick with towers and a mansard roof. Behind were several large outbuildings that had been painted to fade into the landscape. Garages, I decided, and maybe a barn for various landscaping and maintenance machines and tools.

It had a large pool with brilliant flowers and greenery. It was an emerald oasis in a dry summer landscape. Objectively, it was gorgeous and everything a narcissist would want in a house. The design looked enough like Aunty Mommy's estate that I had to wonder if they'd been designed by the same architect. Personally I preferred Luke's place. As big as it was, it still felt like a home. This place felt like a museum.

My phone buzzed and I checked it. "Stacey's here."

"I'll go get her."

"Oh, fuck."

He stopped. "What?"

"She says Mikey's here too. I'd better come with you."

He put a hand on my arm. "I'll handle it. Someone has to find Lydia. You're our secret weapon. You don't have time to get derailed. Plus Lorraine and Jen may need backup. Go do your thing and don't worry about Stacey. I've got her."

I didn't like it, but he was right. I nodded reluctantly. "Do me a favor though."

"What's that?"

"Don't let her near Flannery."

He gave me a *no, duh,* look. "I'm not an idiot." He started to walk away.

"One more thing."

"What?"

"Lindsey told me something bad is coming for me. She didn't say what, when, or how, but there's not a lot worse that could happen than Jen, Lorraine, or Stacey getting hurt. Keep your eyes peeled. Don't let anything happen to her."

His expression turned sober. "I won't. Same to you."

"If anybody tries anything, this place is going up like Chernobyl. Count on it."

He stared. "You can do that?" Then, "That's... not comforting."

"I'm not interested in your comfort, but I can promise one thing."

Warily, "What?"

"If someone comes after me or mine, they're going to become an object lesson."

"After that Chernobyl comment, I'm not sure I want to know what that means."

I smiled a hyena smile. "Trust me, you don't."

# CHAPTER NINE

After Luke departed, I headed into the house. It was crowded, people and employees bustling in and out. A ballroom that opened up on a garden patio contained tables and a couple of buffet lines. A jazz quartet played in the courtyard.

I peeked inside, then moved on, checking every door I could. No signs of the cats or Lydia. Would Flannery be so bold as to bring her here during his party? Stupid question. Of course he would. The man was so full of himself he probably couldn't imagine failing.

"Pride goeth before the fall," I murmured, determined that Flannery would fall. Hopefully I'd be the one shoving him off the not proverbial cliff.

Since he was just the kind of narcissistic asshole who would kidnap or blackmail his ex-wife into returning home, what would he do with her? I realized it depended on whether or not one of his goons had forced her, or if Flannery had managed to coerce her into returning.

If I had to guess, and I did, I'd guess the latter. The asshat was the type to enjoy forcing people to do what he wanted. He wanted to pull the strings and watch them dance, enjoying the fact that they chose to put themselves in his power. I snorted. Chose. Some choice. Hey Lydia, I'll slowly cut apart your cats until they die and make you watch, or you can come back and live in luxury and be my obedient political wife.

I'd bet a blowjob that the conversation had gone pretty much just like that. Which meant that Lydia would have entered the house of her own free will and wouldn't need to be locked up or guarded.

Realization struck me. She'd be in the owner's suite. Flannery meant for her to go back to being his wife, and that would include sex. He'd also want to make sure she was constantly reminded of what would happen if she failed to perform. He'd like watching her squirm, watching her fear and submission. Fucker.

His predictability was good for me, however, since that meant he'd have the cats nearby. Lydia wouldn't leave without them, and I wasn't about to leave them in Flannery's hands.

A memory of Ajax and the horrific shape he was in when I rescued him flashed through my mind, and it occurred to me to wonder what had convinced Lydia to come back now. A chill ran through me. What had Flannery done?

I should have gone looking for Lorraine and Jen, or at least texted them, but the memory of Ajax spurred me to action. It didn't make sense. Whatever Flannery had done to the cats was over and done, and I could do nothing, but I was running on instinct and emotion.

The house was huge, but the owner's suite wouldn't be on the first floor and probably not the second. Those would likely be reserved for guests. The best views were on the third floor, which was probably the family floor. The fourth was probably storage spaces, offices, art studios, or something along those lines. Private places for the family where guests weren't allowed.

Security guarded the two elevators at either end of the house. I expected there was another freight elevator somewhere, but likely it was guarded, too. I went in search of a back stairs, keeping an eye out for Jen and Lorraine. Because I'd cast the glamour on them, I wouldn't have trouble seeing them.

A pair of women stopped to admire me. Both were likely in their thirties or early forties and had dressed with effortless elegance. I'd named my business—Effortless Estates—after just that kind of fashionable perfection that seemed perfectly natural.

"You look stunning in that dress," the first one gushed. She was thicker around the middle with large breasts, and wore a layered, blue-gray chiffon dress that set off her pale skin and strawberry blonde hair. It was perfectly cut and complimented her figure.

"I'd love to get the name of the designer," the other said. She was tall, with wide shoulders and a straight waist. She wore a slip dress made of layered silk that flattered her figure. A bootie-pump hybrid in calfskin and dyed the same pinkish-gray as her dress completed her look. Her hair was brown with expensive honey highlights.

Both women looked flawless and expensive. Just the kind of clients Rhi and Lorel needed.

"Thank you," I said. "Her name is Rhiannon Larson. She's very exclusive, but if you have a card, I can pass it along for you."

They dug out their cards and passed them to me. "I've

got a function soon and I'd love to wear something by her," slip dress said.

"I'd love to get a holiday dress or two from her," chiffon dress added.

"I'll pass along your information as soon as I can. Could you direct me toward a bathroom?"

Soon I found myself just inside a bathroom sitting area where women gazed at themselves in mirrors and reapplied their makeup, or simply sat in the comfortable sitting area to cool down after the outside heat. I stood for a moment, ignoring the curious looks I got and then stepped back outside. Instead of turning back toward the party, I went the other way, hoping it would lead me to the service areas.

I finally found a laundry room with two sets of industrial washers and dryers. Folding tables ran down one wall, along with stacks of baskets and rolling carts. Shelves loaded with cleaning supplies covered another wall.

The freight elevator had to be near in order to transport the laundry up and down, and the stairs would likely be close to it. When I found the freight elevator, I was pleasantly surprised to discover it wasn't guarded at all. I pressed the button, and it opened instantly. I stepped inside and hit the button for the third floor. Just as the doors started to slide shut, Jen and Lorraine came flying inside.

Adrenaline spiked along with fear. "What's the matter? Who's after you?"

"Nobody," Jen said. "We saw you and didn't want to yell and draw attention to you, so we ran down the stairs and jumped aboard."

"Where are you going? You're supposed to be distracting Flannery," Lorraine said.

"I realized Lydia has to be here in the house," I said, and quickly explained my logic.

Lorraine and Jen exchanged horrified looks as the elevator stopped at the third floor. The doors slid open. We looked out and found ourselves standing in a small vestibule. A door on the other side led into a large janitorial closet. A single hallway led out.

"Let us go ahead," Jen told me. "We're not noticeable. You are."

I'd considered casting a glamour on myself but didn't figure I needed to. If anybody saw me, I'd just hit them with magic and knock them cold.

Lorraine motioned me closer as she and Jen glanced down the cross hallway.

"Where should we look first?" she asked.

"We should split up," I said.

Jen gave me a sharp look. "What aren't you telling us?"

I shook my head. "I just have this feeling." That's when I remembered Flannery's phone call after he'd left Luke and I. "Flannery came in the house," I said. "He got a call and came straight here."

"Which means he's probably with Lydia," Jen said.

"I really don't like the sound of that," Lorraine said darkly.

"Me, either. He's got to be angry that she made him look bad by leaving and then wouldn't come crawling back. He's going to want revenge or to teach her a lesson, or both. I'm betting he'll start on the cats and then graduate to her."

"We'd better find her fast, then," Jen said. "He could kill her and nobody would know she was even here. *We* don't even know for sure."

"She's here," I said confidently.

"I believe you but would the cops? He really could

decide to kill her to keep her from being a problem. Or just lose his temper and go too far. Let's go find her."

Jen and Lorraine went left, splitting up where the hallway joined another. I went right. The upstairs was as much of a maze as downstairs, but with more rooms. I didn't bother looking inside any of the doors I passed. The owner's suite would have an imposing entrance. None of these rooms fit. If I were building the house, I'd put the owner's suite on the north or south end. Both would have a three quarter view of the surrounding terrain, and you'd be able to watch both the sunrise and sunset if you wanted.

I didn't hear any screaming or crying, which I took as a positive, and then remembered he could easily have sound-proofed his room. Many people did so for good reasons, though I had no doubt Flannery's were putrid. *If* he'd soundproofed.

Pulling off my shoes to move more quickly, I trotted through the winding corridors, making as much of a beeline for where I imagined Flannery must be holding Lydia as I could. I didn't see the maid and crashed into her, sending her tray of empty dishes flying.

"Oh!" I staggered and caught myself against the wall, turning around to face her. "Are you all right?"

She'd fallen against the opposite wall. She straightened, turning an accusing look on me. "What are you doing here? This area is private." She smoothed her hands over her uniform, wrinkling her nose as her fingers smeared something that looked like jelly.

"Have you seen Carson Flannery? Or Lydia Flannery? Where is their suite?"

She goggled at me. "Why would Mrs. Flannery be here? She up and deserted poor Mr. Flannery. She broke his heart."

"She may have snuck in," I said. "Someone said they saw her coming up this way."

The maid's eyes rounded. "She wouldn't."

"I'd hate for her to ruin Carson's party," I said with a concerned look. "Or worse." I let her imagine what worse could be. It would probably be better than anything I could come up with.

When she still wavered, I went in for the kill. "You don't think she'd hurt him, do you?"

That did it. She gasped and spun in the opposite direction. I followed as she flung open a room, ran through it and a bathroom and then out into another hallway. She jogged right and then left, and suddenly the owner's suite was right in front of us.

It wasn't as imposing as I'd have thought. In keeping with the French chateau look, the small vestibule outside contained a Louis XVI couch and two chairs painted white and upholstered in blue, two marble round marble topped tables with glass vases full of fresh white gladiolas and roses.

The white doors leading into the suite were paneled and at least ten feet tall.

"Should I get security?"

I shook my head. "Not yet. Let me just check to see if anything's amiss. We wouldn't want to embarrass Carson if nothing was wrong, or if the woman someone saw wasn't Mrs. Flannery."

She nodded and chewed her lower lip.

I went to check the door. I tapped on the door. "Carson? It's me, Rebecca. Are you inside?"

If his room was soundproofed, he wouldn't hear. I noticed a discreet button set in the wainscoting just to the left of the door. The maid clearly wasn't aware of it. I shifted to block her view of it and now I knocked hard, raising my voice.

"Carson? Are you there? Are you okay?"

Once again he didn't answer, and I pretended to look chagrined. I needed to get in, and I needed her to stay out of the way.

"I'm really sorry about this," I said, and hit her with a spell Damon had been teaching me. It was meant to be defensive—a way to knock out an attacker and give you time to get away. Considering the fact that the attackers he feared were all witches and would be shielded against a knock-out spell, it was a pretty pointless lesson. I hadn't argued, though, since it *could* be useful, and it made him feel better. I'd been able to get a handle on it pretty quickly, largely because it didn't require complicated spell work I still didn't understand.

The maid crumpled to the rug-covered slate, and I winced. The rug was made of piled wool, but she was still going to wake up with a headache and bruises.

Cue Jen's and Lorraine's arrival.

"What's going on?" Jen asked as Lorraine bent to check the maid's pulse.

"I knocked her out. With magic," I added when Lorraine started looking for a lump. "She should be fine."

"She's got a good pulse and is breathing steady." Lorraine pushed to her feet.

"Should we move her?" Jen asked, frowning at the girl's prone body.

"We need to make sure Lydia's okay first." Even as I said it, I went to the door and tried the knobs. Locked. Not a problem. With a jolt of magic, I softened the locking mechanism and pushed on the door. A little resistance and they parted, swinging silently open.

I went inside first, gaze sweeping the darkened interior. The drapes were shut and the lights off. It was difficult to make out more than the hunched shadows of furniture and decorations.

I heard the rumble of Flannery's voice and a shriek followed by his laughter. I followed the sounds, careful not to make any noise of my own. Jen and Lorraine followed close on my heels.

We left the first room and passed through two others until we arrived at a massive bathroom like none I'd ever seen.

"Holy shit," Lorraine whispered.

"Buy this house, Beck. We need it," Jen added in quiet awe.

The bathroom—the name did not give it justice—was a large round room with a ceiling that went all the way up to the roof, where a skylight allowed in a fall of light. Along one wall was a massive counter with two waterfall sinks, the cabinets all made of polished teak. Dominating the space was a glassed-in garden where a stone tub big enough for five people had been sunk in the floor. Rainfall showers interspersed the plants, along with benches and chairs. The floor was a mix of smooth stone and moss. A tree stretched its limbs up toward the skylight.

As pretty as it all was, we swiftly realized Flannery had turned it into a garden of horrors.

Lydia stood beside the tub wearing only her bra and panties. Flannery had tied her hands and thrown the rope over a tree limb and pulled it taut, so that her arms were extended above her head. He'd also tied ropes to her ankles and secured the ropes to a couple of stone seats. She was crying and begging him to let her go.

"You know better than that, Lydia," he told her as he

walked behind her. He'd removed his jacket and rolled up his sleeves, and held what looked like a riding crop. "You've been very naughty and you'll need to apologize to me for all the trouble you've caused, and then you'll need to be an exemplary wife. That's why you're here, isn't it? You didn't have to come. I gave you a choice, and you *wanted* to come back home.

"Now this first is going to be rough, I won't lie. Nobody knows you're here, and nobody is going to see you, so I can leave marks, and I plan to. I need to make sure that you understand what happens when you defy me. You've embarrassed me, and that's just unacceptable. You need to show me you understand, and the only way to do that is to beg me to punish you for your transgressions. I've been too patient, too giving, and you took advantage by running away.

I looked at Jen. "Call Mikey. If he doesn't take you seriously, call Ballard and Jeffers." The latter two had investigated my Aunty Mommy's murder. Hopefully Mikey chose to take Jen seriously, as he was already outside somewhere and could be upstairs in the bathroom within minutes.

She withdrew, and I dug in my pocket for my phone and handed it to Lorraine. "Lydia is going to need evidence. Get it for her. Record what you can."

I went back to watching. There wasn't a snowball's chance in hell Mikey would get here before Flannery got serious about beating Lydia, and I wasn't going to watch her suffer just so they could see his violence for themselves. The video would have to be enough. I gritted my teeth. I'd have to let him hit her once or twice so that he couldn't say he was just playacting or whatever excuse he'd come up with. He already had the cops and his political cronies on his side. Any chance to let him off the hook and they'd take it.

Not on my watch.

I called up my magic, holding it ready and willing Lydia to hold on and be strong.

"I haven't heard you apologize, yet, Lydia."

She mumbled something through her tears. He hit her so fast I didn't realize he had until he'd struck three or four times. He slashed the whip across her stomach and breasts. She screamed and twisted and begged him to stop and broke into a repeated chant of 'sorry.' He grabbed her hair and pulled her head up and back, staring down into her face.

"Speak up, wife. The longer it takes for you to learn your lessons, the more it's going to hurt. I don't want to punish you, but how else will you learn? I hope you appreciate how hard this is for me. I wish you'd treated me better, so I wouldn't have to do this. It is what it is, though, so we'll just have to grin and bear it."

He bent and kissed her, forcing her mouth open, letting go of her hair and grasping her jaw, digging his fingers into her flesh to hold her still. He finished by biting her lower lip and pulling it with his teeth. She moaned and he let go. Blood dribbled down her chin, mixing with snot and tears.

"Isn't that enough?" Lorraine whispered. "I can't take much more of this."

What did law enforcement need to see, so they couldn't ignore the situation this time? What would it take for them to put Flannery behind bars? I didn't know. What I did know was that the news stations would eat this up. Flannery's political career was over. That was nice, but I wanted more. I wanted her safe. A video might not even be enough, and that left the guarantee up to me and my magic. I knew just the incentive he needed to stay away.

I cleared my throat and walked into the glassed-in garden. "Hello again, Carson," I said as if he wasn't standing there holding a whip beside the mostly naked woman he'd been beating.

He went feral as weasels do when they are trapped. "What are you doing here?" he snarled. "How did you get in? I locked the doors."

I shrugged. "I unlocked them."

"How? Nobody has a key but me."

"Is that really what you want to talk about? I don't. I want to know why you've imprisoned your wife and are beating her." I kept my voice conversational. I wanted to give Jen time to summon Mikey and his cop buddies. Their arrival would feed the scandal of the video when we leaked it. I wanted his political aspirations dead and rotting.

"This is none of your business. It's between me and my wife, and she's here of her own free will. Ask her," he said defiantly.

"Is that true, Lydia? Do you want to be tied up and whipped?"

She went still and then gave a slow nod.

"See?" he demanded triumphantly.

"I do see," I said. "You stole her cats and threatened to kill or mutilate them. To keep them safe, she's agreed to let you abuse her however you want."

I half expected him to argue, but he didn't see Lorraine recording him. Even if he had, I don't know that he'd have been able to keep his mouth shut. Some people have no sense of self preservation. Not that I was complaining.

"Personally I could care less about a cat, but Lydia here —" He rubbed the tip of the whip over her collar bone, between her breasts, and then snapped it against her belly. "—Lydia's got a soft spot for those damned things, and they don't even belong to her. I bought them for her for her birthday."

"If you gave them as a gift, legally they're hers, are they not?" I pointed out.

"Not at all. She belongs to me, and that means everything she calls hers belongs to me, too. I own her clothes, her shoes, her make-up, her jewelry, and the damned cats. I own these tits, this sweet ass, and that tight cunt of hers." As he spoke, he groped each body part in turn. "She has no right to refuse anything I want. If she does, I'm within my rights as a husband and a man to take what belongs to me. I'm not only within my rights, it's my duty to put her on the right path."

"So you'll rape her."

"It's not rape if she's my wife. She should want to please me. It's her failure as a woman if she doesn't."

"Do you really believe this shit you're spewing?"

He took a step closer, his gaze running over me like I was meat on the hoof. "It's how things work. I could teach you a thing or two about pleasing your man."

"No thanks. There's not enough acid in the world to clean your foul touch off me."

Just at that moment, Jen returned. "They'll be here in a minute," she told me, then shifted her attention to Flannery. "Do you suppose he has a tiny dick, and he's doing all this to compensate?"

"Most likely," I replied. "Lorraine, what do you think?"

She stepped out of the shadows, still holding my phone up and recording. "Seems reasonable," she said. "His pants certainly have plenty of room in the crotch, like he doesn't have much to fill them"

Flannery scowled. "Who are you talking to?" His gaze ran over Jen and Lorraine and slid past like he didn't see them.

Right. The glamour. Wasn't a lot of use for it anymore. I decided to dissolve it. I brushed a finger over Lorraine's shoulder and then across Jen's wrist, pulling the magic back inside me.

"Where did she come from?" Flannery demanded, now that he was able to focus on Lorraine. "And her. Who are they? What are they doing here? Why are they dressed like cat burglars?"

I'll admit I laughed at that one. "They dressed for success," I said.

"What the fuck does that mean? And who's coming?" He scowled at Lorraine, who was still recording. "Put that damned phone down. I'll sue your asses from here to China and back for breach of privacy, trespassing, and everything else I can think of. By the time I'm done with you, you'll be broke in a gutter and wishing you'd never met me."

"We already wish we'd never met you," Jen said. "In answer to your question, the police are on their way."

He smiled with a certainty that made me want to punch it right off his face. "Good. Saves me the trouble."

"Mr. Flannery? Is everything all right? What—?" The maid had regained consciousness and now stood just inside the bathroom. Her eyes went wide. and her mouth fell open as she took in the scene. "What's going on?" she whispered finally.

"Your boss is a psychopath," Jen told her. "And a wife-beater, not to mention an asshole. He's going to be going to jail, so you may want to look for another job."

"Police are on their way," I told her. Mikey was probably waiting for backup. "Why don't you go escort them up?"

She nodded and slowly backed out of the doorway.

I waited until she was gone before addressing Flannery. "There are just one or two things we've got to take care of before the police arrive. You see, I don't entirely trust the cops to do the right thing. Sometimes the law ties their hands; sometimes they can't find the evidence they need; sometimes they just fuck up. So I'm going to punish you, just like you were going to punish Lydia. You don't have to agree to it, either. Just know that you've been found guilty and given a life sentence."

"Sure, do your worst," he said with a smirk.

Even Lorraine putting away my phone didn't shake his cockiness. So what if we didn't want the next bit recorded? In his shoes, I probably would have felt the same. What could I possibly do to him? Put sugar in his gas tank? Pour motor oil on his lawn? Toilet paper his house?

I'd originally planned a hellish inconvenience for him. I was going to curse him so that any clothes or shoes he put on would instantly shrink a size. He'd perpetually have to deal with too small clothes. That was before, when I thought he was just a nuisance. That wasn't going to cut it now. He needed to learn a lesson, and I was going to teach it to him.

I collected my thoughts, focused, and released my magic.

# CHAPTER TEN

It was remarkably satisfying to watch the smirk slide off Flannery's face, replaced by confusion. While he sorted through what was happening to him, I sliced through Lydia's leg shackles with magic.

I strode over to her. "Hi Lydia. I'm Beck. I'm a friend of Stacey's from the club. I'm going to release you, but I don't want to hurt you. Will you be able to stand on your own?"

Her body shifted. She straightened and lifted her head, looking at me through the tangle of her hair. Her pale brown eyes glittered with anger. I stared. She'd been so wilted and destroyed, the sudden shift caught me off guard.

"If you let me down, I'll kill him," she said in a stone-hard voice, completely opposite to the helpless weeping woman she'd appeared to be just moments before.

"No, you won't," I said. "You're not going to let him win, and he will if you go to jail for murder."

"He deserves to be dead," she spat.

"Preaching to the choir, but you don't deserve to pay for it. Are you ready? I'm going to cut the ropes." I waited for her nod, and then she was free.

She squeaked and sagged at the suddenness of her freedom. I caught her around the waist and she sucked in a sharp breath as I touched a sore spot. I wondered what he'd done to her before we got there.

"Steady now," I said. "Tell me when you are ready to stand."

"How did you do that?"

"You wouldn't believe me if I told you."

"I'm okay," she said after a moment. "You can let go."

I slowly released her, staying close in case she started to fall.

"Here." Lorraine came into the glass enclosure. She held out a light-weight robe.

"Thanks." Lydia took it. Her hands shook. She winced as she moved to put the robe on. "Fuck, but that hurts."

"Sorry," I said, guilt surging. "I could have stopped him sooner but thought we should get some video so you'd have proof for the cops."

She gave an adamant shake of her head. "Don't apologize. You're right. If I'm ever going to be free of him, I need to be able to show the world just what kind of man he is."

"Why pretend to be scared and broken?" Lorraine asked curiously.

"He's a coward. He likes to talk. He always talks more when I'm not sassing him. I hoped I'd get lucky, and he'd give me some kind of ammunition." She looked at me as she tied the robe around herself. "I'm more grateful than I can say for you stepping in." She made a face. "The cops are going to call me stupid for coming back to him just to protect my cats, though. It probably was fucking stupid."

I shook my head. "I get it. I'd have done the same."

She gave me a distrusting look. "You don't have to say that. I know how ridiculous it was. A couple of cats don't matter as much as I do. Except for me, they do. I knew he wasn't going to kill me, though. He's always had a thing for hurting me. He likes it when I cry and beg."

The way she said it struck me hard. It reminded me of the way I talked about what Aunty Mommy had done to me. Like it was just the way things were, and I had to deal with it because it wasn't changing. Only I'd been wrong and so had Lydia. Aunty Mommy got herself killed, and Lydia made friends with Stacey. I couldn't do anything about my torturer, but I could do something about Lydia's.

"Anyhow, I wasn't going to let him hurt my cats, and I figured that if I escaped with them once, I could do it again, and this time I'd figure out how to disappear." She sighed. "It *was* stupid. I should have at least thought of a better plan, but I didn't have time. I had to come immediately or he'd…"

She trailed off and swallowed.

"No judgment here," I said softly.

"It's just that Carson only came after the cats because of me. I had to try to help them. They wouldn't be in the situation if not for me."

"You don't owe me any explanations," I assured her. "I really do get it. I dealt with my own abuser. She threatened my friends, and trust me, I'd have done anything to keep them out of her clutches."

"But that was people. I did this for cats. The police aren't going to take me seriously. Again."

"They will. We have video, and you've got witnesses."

"Right." She squared her shoulders and tossed the hair out of her face. "This time is going to be different."

"Fucking right it will be," Jen said.

She and Lorraine had stepped inside the enclosure.

"What's with the fuckwit?" Lorraine asked. "What did you do to him?"

I considered my handiwork. Flannery looked panicked and was looking down at himself.

"Something wrong?" I asked.

He looked at me. "What did you do to me? Is it some kind of poison?"

I was tempted to tell him to figure it out himself, but I had time to gloat and make him aware of his new limitations. I decided to indulge myself.

"If this were a fairytale, and if I were a witch intent on distributing appropriate justice as often happens in fairy tales, I would say that you're suffering a physical manifestation of your shitty thoughts. That every time you even think of hurting Lydia in any possible way, your dick will start burning, and you'll get an insanely itchy and painful rash. It'll spread over your balls and out along your body and won't go away until you've willingly sat and endured it for at least twenty four hours. The ticking clock resets every time you think about her again."

I shrugged. "But of course, that's just a fairytale. That sort of thing doesn't happen in the real world, so I have no idea what's going on with you. Maybe you should see a doctor, though I've heard that conditions like this can plague you for the rest of your life. Oh, and don't imagine you'll be able to get out of it by committing suicide. You can try, but killing yourself won't take."

I glanced at Lydia, who was looking at me like I should be wearing a straitjacket. "Is that the sort of punishment you'd inflict if you could? Or would you add to that? I mean, if you could curse him with something."

Her gaze narrowed. "I'm grateful for you rescuing me, but I don't appreciate you making fun of my situation."

"I'm not," I said. "Just tell me, in the best of all possible worlds, what would you do to pay him back for what he's done?"

"I don't know. I'd want to make sure he didn't hurt another woman again. Or an animal. Or anybody, really."

I nodded. "I should have thought of that. Good call."

I focused, gathering my magic and shaping my intent. I lobbed the spell at him.

"Is that it?" Jen asked.

"I thought it would be more... noticeable," Lorraine said, disappointment twining through her voice.

"Kick him in the balls and see what happens," I suggested.

"I'd love to," Lorraine said. "But Lydia deserves to do that one."

"Want to kick him in the nuts, Lydia?" I asked her.

Confusion, irritation, and pain mingled on her face. "I don't understand what's going on here."

"I know, and if the cops get here first, you won't get a chance to give him a taste of his own medicine," I said. "What do you have to lose?"

"Blood?"

"Worth a risk, though, isn't it?" I asked "If it were me, I'd take that crop and beat him bloody, then stomp on him until I broke every bone in his body." I shrugged. "It's probably over the top, but I'm vindictive that way."

She hesitated, then crossed over to where he stood and plucked the crop from his hand. He snarled and reached out to grab her by the throat. She flinched away even as he staggered back, his mouth opening and closing as he struggled for air. He retreated another two steps and was able to suck in a loud breath before breaking into coughs.

"What happens if he tries to, say, shoot someone?" Jen asked in the same tone she'd order coffee.

"He'll suffer the fate he intends, just short of dying. If he decides to poison someone, he'll feel the effects of the poison all the way to the point of death, and then he'll recover. Same for a shooting or trying to choke someone."

"You can't be serious," Lydia said, staring at Flannery as the coughing fit faded, and he straightened, looking a little sick and scared, like he'd finally figured out something strange was in play, and he wasn't weaseling out of paying for his actions this time. "For fuck's sake. What am I even saying? That's impossible. It's crazy!"

"You'd think, but humor us. Try it again," Jen said. "If it works twice, it's probably true."

Lydia studied her for a moment, and finally nodded, clearly dubious. She lifted the crop high, and Flannery grabbed for her arm, only to yelp and clutch his own as he tried to back out of reach.

"Fucking bitch!"

Still holding the crop high, Lydia pursued him. "Nobody asked you for your opinion, so keep it to yourself," she said and brought it down with a whistling *thwack*! The crop stuck across his crotch and upper thighs.

He howled and grabbed himself, bending over.

Lydia's eyes widened, and she gave a delighted laugh. "Stand up again, you good for nothing piece of shit. You've got a lot more coming."

"And here's the drunk with power portion of the show," Lorraine said.

"She's more than allowed," I said.

"Damned straight," Lorraine said. "It's kind of nice to see a woman turn the tables for once."

"My thoughts exactly."

Flannery still hadn't accepted his new reality. He shook a fist at Lydia. "You're going to regret this, bitch. You'll never be free of me. I'll make your life miserable until Doomsday."

Even as he said it, he gasped and made a squawking noise then scratched himself furiously as a bubbly red rash spread from under his clothing across his exposed skin. It looked like poison oak on steroids.

"That looks unpleasant," Jen noted.

"I did my best," I said.

"I think the cavalry's arrived," Lorraine said, turning to listen.

With the place sound-proofed, the only noise came in through the main door of the suite, which could no longer close thanks to me.

I heard the thud of footsteps and clank of metal on metal. Several cops in uniform with guns raised entered the outer part of the bathroom and spread out, followed by Officer Mikey who strolled in.

"Everybody stand still," he ordered.

Jen snorted. "Because we were in the middle of running a marathon," she muttered, rolling her eyes.

I snickered, and Mikey scowled. His own fault. If he was going to leave a door that wide open, somebody was bound to step through.

"What's going on here?" he demanded after examining the tableau.

"I'll tell you what's happened," Flannery declared, stomping toward the doorway of the glass enclosure, only to come to a halt in front of Jen and Lorraine, who declined to move. He started to push forward with every intention of shouldering them out of his way, but magic shoved him backward, and he sprawled onto his ass.

Lydia barked out a laugh. "Carson, I've never seen you look better. Stay there, why don't you."

He let out a string of epithets and struggled to his feet. "I want these people arrested for trespassing, breaking and entering, and assault. They've done something to me. It's some sort of chemical like anthrax or Agent Orange. I need to see a doctor right away. Call an ambulance."

"Or," I said. "You could arrest Flannery for unlawful imprisonment and assault, plus being an all-around asshole. Then take him to the hospital if he wants, though I'm pretty sure they can't help with his particular problem." I looked at him. "You are such a coward. You can dish it out, but you can't take it. Best learn fast."

"That's a little harsh," Lorraine said. "It's not like he can help it. Poor dear only has two brain cells, and they're fighting hard for third place."

Jen snickered.

"Maybe someone could explain what's going on," Mikey said, his tone indicating it wasn't the suggestion it sounded like.

"This is Lydia, Flannery's ex," I said. "Try not to ignore her, this time, would you?"

The other woman's mouth tightened, and she clearly didn't want anything to do with the police. I couldn't reassure her. Mikey was a wild card. He could easily go the asshole route or could actually listen. He'd seemed to thaw into a decent human last night with Lindsey, but breakfast this morning had him freezing right back up. Not that he hadn't had a good point or two, but he hadn't been particularly supportive.

"Ma'am?" Mikey said. "Could you tell me what happened here?"

She curled her lip. "Fine, but I'm not putting up with

anyone treating me like I'm some scorned housewife out for revenge. If you'd paid the slightest attention to me when I told you what my husband was up to, I wouldn't be here."

"Yes, ma'am. Maybe we could talk in another room, where you'll be more comfortable," Mikey suggested as she came out of the enclosure. He looked at one of the uniformed cops. "Take these four where they can wait but don't let them talk to each other. Please follow me, Mrs. Flannery."

"I go by Bishop now."

"Is that so? Are you divorced?"

She grimaced, holding tight to the edge of her borrowed robe. "No such luck, I'm afraid. Maybe soon."

He ushered her out and we followed, with Flannery bringing up the rear. The uniforms led us into a small sitting room where two of them took up stations inside and two guarded outside. Overkill, much?

I sat down on a small settee. It bore a similar look to the furniture in the vestibule outside the suite's doors. Lorraine and Jen sat on either side of me.

"This is fun," Jen said, watching Flannery pace and scratch and mutter.

"No talking, please," the female uniform called out.

"Nap time, I guess," I murmured, and slid off the settee onto the floor, grabbed a throw pillow off another chair, stuffed it under my head, and closed my eyes.

Jen woke me up a while later. I jerked up, adrenaline spiking through me. A throwback to dealing with Aunty Mommy. The combination of sleeping on the floor and somebody shaking me awake put me right back in that headspace.

I sucked in a breath as I realized where I was. I blew it out slowly, blinking away the grittiness in my eyes.

"You okay?" Lorraine asked.

I nodded. "Just startled." And half expecting a kick to the gut, but she didn't need to know that.

"You've been summoned."

I looked around. We were the only two left. "Where's Jen and the assbite?"

"They got called out already. Well, Officer Mike wanted you after Flannery, but Jen went instead. Said you needed sleep."

"And he accepted that?"

"You know how Jen can be. I got the distinct impression nobody wanted to have to shoot her, and they'd have had to if they didn't back down, so she got her way."

"Sounds about right." I got to my feet, remembering I'd thrown my shoes somewhere. I'd have to find them. I wouldn't have cared if they were mine, but they weren't and they were one of a kind.

The female cop who'd been on guard duty stood just a few feet away, listening. Probably why she had let us talk. "A fair assessment," she agreed.

I smoothed my hands over my dress and hair before following her out. She directed me into a larger salon. The furniture within had a more masculine feel—chunky and upholstered in dark leather with decorative brass nails. It all looked handmade.

Mikey leaned against the arm of a couch, flipping through his notebook. He straightened when I came in, the uniform closing the door behind me.

"Have a seat," he said, pointing to one in particular. It faced another chair, where he no doubt planned to sit.

At least they looked comfortable. I went ahead and obeyed. The faster I got through this, the faster I could go help look for the cats.

"I had Lydia taken to the hospital," he said as he settled into his chair. "She's being assessed and treated. I sent a forensic photographer to take pictures of everything."

"Good."

"Just wanted you to know I was on top of it. Flannery will have a tough time weaseling out of this one."

"If you say so." I wasn't feeling particularly charitable. At the moment he represented the system that had so totally failed Lydia. It wasn't fair to make him their figurehead, but I wasn't in the mood to be fair at the moment. "Did anybody find the cats?"

He nodded. "They were in cages in the bedroom."

"They're okay?"

"As far as I can tell. One of them has a bunch of little stripes shaved into its fur. I guess—" He broke off with a grimace. "Not something I should discuss."

"That's how he showed Lydia where he'd cut the cat, wasn't it? He couldn't afford to kill them for real, or he wouldn't have leverage," I mused aloud. "So he shaved where he'd cut so she'd know he was serious."

Mikey smiled appreciatively. "Something along those lines, yes."

"So what do you want to know?"

"I need your version of what happened up here."

My brows rose. "The real one or the sanitized one?"

Another smile. "Real one. I'll take notes on what I need to remember."

Meaning none of the magic. I launched into the story and didn't hold anything back. He didn't interrupt, just nodding now and again as he jotted notes. He snorted a little when I described the spells I'd cast. When I got to the end, he continued writing and then proceeded to read over his notes.

I waited semi-patiently. I was getting hungry and thirsty. I wanted to eat, have a long, hot bath, and then sleep for about a day. And snuggle Ajax. I'd left him at Luke's with Rhi and Lorel to look after him. If I had to guess, he'd crawled into bed with Lindsey as soon as I left.

"You told Jen to call me or Detectives Ballard and Jeffers," Mikey said, not looking up from his notebook.

I didn't respond, and he lifted his gaze to look expectantly at me.

"What?"

"*Did* you tell Jen to call me or Detectives Ballard and Jeffers?"

"Yes."

"Why me?"

I gave him the side-eye, not sure where he was going with this. "Do you want me to apologize or something? I'm sure you could have figured out how to pass on the call if you wanted."

He shook his head, running his hand through his hair. "That's not what I meant."

"What did you mean?"

"Why did you—" He broke off and blew out a breath. "No, that's not it. You knew I was going to do this by the book. I wasn't going to do you any favors."

"We don't need any favors. We just need a little honesty and integrity. Have you seen the video?"

He nodded. "Had a look after Lydia told me about it."

"And?"

"DA won't have a choice. He'll have to charge him. Since it's going to be high-profile, he might even decide to make an example of Flannery."

"Good."

"Thanks."

"For what?"

"Trusting me to be a good cop."

I shrugged. "You are a good cop. That's not what I have issues with."

"So you said. I've got some thinking to do."

"About what?"

"Whether or not I'm as good a cop as I want to be."

I didn't know what to say to that. "Can I go?"

He nodded. "I'll be in touch if I need more information. You'll need to come downtown and make a formal statement, but you can do that Monday. Jen and Lorraine, too."

"What's going to happen to Lydia? And her cats? Can she have them back?"

He nodded. "I don't know if the hospital will keep her overnight, but she'll be able to pick them up. CSU took pictures, so there's no need to keep them."

"What happens if she can't get them tonight?"

"Animal Control will probably take them."

"Or we could. Lorraine's a vet. You could have her check them out, make sure he didn't hurt them."

"That's fine. I'm sure Lydia will appreciate it. I'll clear it with CSU and let her know."

"Thanks."

I headed for the door, stopping just within to look at him. He'd shown there was more to him than I'd thought. I could see some of what drew Stacey to him. "Stacey does want a forever relationship. She just doesn't believe they exist, and she's not willing to risk seeing if they do."

He looked at me in surprise. "I can't tell if you're saying I should keep trying, or if there's no hope for me."

I shrugged. "All I know is you can't win if you don't play. Think hard, though. You can't change her to fit your idea of the perfect woman, any more than she can change you. Either you want her, warts and all, or you don't."

He nodded. "I hear you."

"Look at that. Progress already. Nothing sexier than a man who listens. Nothing harder to find, either."

I waved my fingers at him and left, smiling when I heard him laugh.

Maybe he wasn't as fuckwitted as he'd been acting. Only time would tell.

# CHAPTER ELEVEN

We gathered at Luke's after we escaped from Flannery's party. He'd been perp-walked out in front of all his guests, and even though he was taken to the hospital, it was obvious he was no longer a free man. Videos had been flying onto the net from all the guests who'd managed to capture the moment. With any luck, the video Lorraine had taken would end up there too.

"Couldn't happen to a nicer guy," I said from where I sat on the floor. Ajax lay between my legs with his head pillowed on my thigh. I leaned against the couch where Jen and Stacey sat. Luke sprawled in an overstuffed chair. I lifted my beer toward the TV, where Flannery had just shuffled to the ambulance, hands cuffed, and trying to scratch the incessant itches plaguing him. "May he reap all that he sowed," I said and then took a swallow of my beer.

"Amen," Jen said.

"When does the pizza get here?" Stacey asked. "I haven't eaten all day, and this beer is going straight to my head."

"Best stay away from Luke, then. He's not above seducing you when you're drunk," Jen said.

"You'd stop him," Stacey said confidently.

"Or we'd wave good-bye and tell you to have fun," I said.

She nudged my shoulder with her bare foot. "You wouldn't."

"I might."

"Traitor."

"You've said it many times: orgasms are the best way to release stress."

"Says the woman who's been sharing a bed with a stunningly handsome man and has yet to play ride 'em, cowboy," Jen drawled.

"I have issues," I said.

"And he has blue balls," Luke said. "I can relate."

"As if," Stacey said. "Your sperm turns over faster than condoms at a sex club."

"French fries at McDonalds," I suggested.

"Coffee at Beck's house," Jen added.

"You three are a pain in the ass. Why did I let you into my house again?"

"You're horny and hopeful," Jen said.

A horn honked outside. We jumped up and went to look. Lorraine had returned from checking over Lydia's two Bengal cats. She parked her work truck and hopped out. The pizza delivery car drove up behind her. Luke and Stacey went to grab the pizzas, while Jen helped Lorraine with the cats.

"How are they?" I asked, peeking through the door to admire their unusual spots.

"A little stressed but otherwise good," Lorraine said.

I frowned. "Why is that one so thin?"

Lorraine laughed. "He's not thin. She's fat. Or rather, she's pregnant. She probably has around a month left."

I poked my fingers through the cage to stroke the female behind the ears. "I wonder if Lydia knows."

"If not, she will soon. Mike gave her my number, and she called from the hospital. She's refusing to stay overnight, so she'll be here as soon as she can escape. Grab the litter box and litter, will you? It's on the floor behind my seat."

We went inside and released the cats in a small room, after Ajax investigated their cage and attempted to get his tongue far enough into the cage to bathe them. They weren't scared, but they did seem a little offended. We put down water and canned tuna for them to eat, set up the litter box, and then left them to explore while we dug into the pizza.

"How many people are you planning to feed?" Lorraine asked, eyeing the stack of boxes.

"We wanted some variety," Luke explained. "Plus, you girls eat like horses."

"He's very practiced with his compliments, isn't he?" Jen said, reaching for a plate.

"Truth is sexy, or so I'm told," Luke replied. "Anyhow, you four would laugh in my face and accuse me of trying to get into your pants if I gave you actual compliments."

"Because you would be," Lorraine said.

"True, but I could also be telling the truth. Have you ever thought of that?"

"Maybe," she conceded. "But your track record says you just want to get laid."

We piled our plates and grabbed fresh beers before returning to our seats.

"You know those cats might cause some damage to the furniture and rug, don't you?" Lorraine asked Luke.

He shrugged. "Everything's replaceable. Can't leave them in the cage. They probably haven't been out since Flannery stole them."

"Now see," Jen said, "that's the kind of thing that makes women want you. A good looking guy who likes animals, and doesn't mind them clawing up his expensive belongings. That's like finding a unicorn."

"Don't forget I'm smart and rich," he said, winking.

She grinned. "Most of the time I totally get why Stacey won't have anything to do with you, but every once in a great while I wonder if she's making a mistake. This moment right now is one of those times." She lifted her beer in a silent toast.

"Wow," I said. "I'm not sure I've ever heard you gush about a man like that."

She flipped me off and smiled. "Why don't we talk about you and Damon? What's going on with him?"

My smile slipped a little, and I sighed. "He still hasn't called. I'm beginning to wonder what's going on."

"Do you think something's wrong?" Stacey asked, her brow furrowing.

I shrugged. "I have no idea. I mean, all this business with Lindsey's premonition has me on edge. I have no idea what bad thing could be coming and sure, I wonder if it has something to do with Damon."

"Why don't you call him?" Lorraine asked. "Resolve your worries with a simple conversation. Grown-ups do it all the time. I bet you could, too."

I stuck my tongue out at her.

"See?" Stacey said. "Sucks when your own friends use logic against you. Call him now."

"Fine." I pulled my phone out and hit the speed dial. The phone rang awhile and then went to voicemail. I almost hung up without leaving a message but stopped myself.

"Hey, Damon," I began and winced. Weak. "It's me, Beck. I'm just touching base to see if everything's okay. Call me when you get a chance." I hung up.

"That was cold," Luke said. "Are you sure he's your boyfriend? Sounds more like the kind of message you'd leave for your dentist."

"Fuck you," I said, quite eloquently, I thought.

"He's not wrong," Lorraine said, ducking when I threw a piece of pineapple at her.

"Gotta agree," Jen said, and Stacey nodded.

"I don't even want to know what you think I should have said."

"Maybe that you miss him? That's pretty basic," Lorraine said.

"Fine. Next time I will tell him I miss him."

"You could always sext him," Luke suggested. "Send pictures or dirty talk."

Jen sighed. "You're such a guy."

"So I know what I'm talking about."

"I am officially done with this conversation," I said. "Next topic, please."

"You still haven't seen the stuff Lindsey wrote while she was having that vision, have you?" Stacey asked.

I shook my head. "No, not yet. Was going to check it out after we finish eating, or maybe after I nap."

Rhi and Lorel had taken Lindsey back to their house, telling me they'd call in a few days when she was feeling back to normal. At the moment, she seemed committed to her imitation of Rip Van Winkle.

"You'll look after eating," Stacey decreed. "Her writings might be time sensitive."

At that, the rest of us broke into laughter.

"What?"

I gasped for air and slowly got myself under control.

"I don't see what's so funny." Stacey eyed us with undisguised annoyance.

"Time sensitive psychic vision," I explained.

"Yeah?"

"It's funny. Like saying the prophecies in Indiana Jones were time sensitive."

"It's not the same thing at all. Lindsey said something bad was coming, and then within hours she had another vision that seems to be related to you. It grabs her so tightly that she spends hours and hours frantically sketching out everything she's seeing, and you don't think there might be some urgency there?"

No, I hadn't thought of that. In fact, I'd been avoiding thinking that. I wanted a small break before the next pile of shit hit the fan. No such luck. I nodded. "You're right."

"Of course I am."

"Maybe I'll look now," I said, setting my plate aside. "Where is the gym?"

"I'll show you," Luke said. "Follow me."

I got up. Ajax eyed me as if trying to decide whether he needed to stand, or if I'd be sitting back down. Concluding that I was, indeed, leaving the room, he jumped up and trotted after me.

"Hold on," Jen said. "We're coming too."

Luke walked into his gym. I stopped on the threshold and just stared, the air going out of my lungs and my mouth drying like the Sahara Desert. I didn't understand what I was looking at; I didn't understand what it said or what it meant. What I did know was that Lindsey had written her scrawling vision in spell language.

Foreboding clutched my lungs. Something very bad was coming. Now I knew for sure it involved witches. Which ones? My parents? Damon? Someone else? What were they after? And more importantly, what were they willing to do to get it?

"Beck?" The girls had squeezed past me and stood looking at me in concern.

"What's wrong?" Jen asked. "You look like someone brained you with a frying pan."

I could only wish. I liked to tell myself that I wasn't going to let any witch grab me, or use me, or do anything to me I didn't want. But the truth was, even though I had a lot of power, that didn't make me strong enough to stand against someone who'd decided they wanted me and were willing to go to any length to make that happen. I didn't know shit about creating spells, I didn't have a lot of experience using my magic, and I had a lot of enemies, most of whom I didn't know. In all truth, I was pretty much a sitting duck.

If someone kidnapped one of the girls or Ajax or Damon, the way Flannery had taken Lydia's cats, I would do almost anything to get them back. I'd let them beat me with riding crops; I'd let them use me as a broodmare; I'd give up my freedom and everything I held dear if it would keep them safe.

I absently rubbed my hand over the bandage on my arm hiding Aunt Mitzi's bite. I hadn't seen her coming any more than I'd foreseen Garrett coming after me. If my history ran true to form, I wouldn't see my next enemy coming.

"I think I need to move to Aunty Mommy's estate," I told them, my voice sounding eerily calm and hollow. "I think you three need to move there too. The gargoyles will protect us until we can figure this out."

I hoped so, anyhow. I'd ask and hope to hell they were willing. And Damon. Suddenly I wanted him back here and safe. I needed to warn him. Maybe he'd have some idea of what Lindsey's scribbles meant.

For a moment, nobody spoke.

"Beck," Lorraine said softly, reaching for my hand. "Until we figure what out?"

I shook my head slowly, feeling dazed. "Who is out to get me. I'm just not sure I can count that high."

THE END

**Keep reading for an exciting excerpt from Beck's next adventure, *Putting the Ice in Nice*!**

# PUTTING THE ICE IN NICE
## EXCERPT

I was cursed.

Again.

I had to be. No one could possibly *not* be cursed and still get a ticket, have a flat tire, *and* spill her triple espresso mocha all over herself and her car before eight in the morning.

I gripped my steering wheel hard, tapping my foot as I waited for the cop to do whatever he was doing. Probably jerking off. He'd taken my license and registration and retreated to the squad car parked behind me, lights flashing red and blue. Cars whizzed by on the highway, some honking gleefully at me. I snarled, tempted to give the last one a flat tire. Or two. Or all of them. I could send a quick zap of magic and the assbite would be hating life at least as much as I was at the moment. I resisted the urge, silently congratulating the lucky bastard on getting away.

Sighing, I tipped my head back against the headrest, closing my eyes and trying to relax. I *had* been speeding. No point arguing. Of course, I'd also been wildly squirming in my seat as hot coffee broiled my thighs and crotch. Good thing sex wasn't on the menu any time soon; I probably had ninth degree burns on my cooch.

If the cop was any kind of a decent human being, he'd have at least considered letting me off with a warning. As it was, he'd barely hidden his laugh when I'd jumped out of the car and performed the hot coffee shimmy and shake, loudly cursing all the while. Now I had to sit in wet pants and underwear as I waited for my ticket. If I did the little nose twitch thing (that's not really how magic works, incidentally) and was suddenly dry, he'd probably be a little curious. Maliciously so.

That was not the way cut the timer on this particular humiliation.

Another sigh and a little smile.

Officer Smug had fast lost his little urge to laugh at me when Ajax had leaped out my open door. He came up to my waist and weighed a good buck-fifty and I could still feel his ribs just a bit when I pet him. He also resembled a wolf. Some even said he was a wolf. I didn't see it. He was a giant, snuggly teddy bear. I'd rescued him from a seriously abusive situation and we'd been close to inseparable since.

Upon Ajax's sudden appearance, Officer Smug had back-pedaled fast, nearly tripping over his own feet. He'd managed not to fall on his ass, so he had no real reason to be pissed. What kind of a man couldn't take a little justified cackling? Anyway, I hadn't turned him into a frog for finding my hot-coffee dance amusing, so he should return the favor and let me go without the ticket.

Though to be fair, he'd have to know of my largesse and telling him I was a witch would probably having him calling the little men in white coats to take me off to the nuthouse. That or he'd have corrected me and said it was spelled b-i-t-c-h.

Asshole.

I dug my fingers into Ajax's ruff and scratched his neck. He gave a little moan and leaned into the caress, lifting his head to give me better access to a particularly itchy spot. I obliged the silent demand, watching Officer Numb-nuts clamber out of his car in the rearview, my left foot tapping impatiently.

I hated being late, even if I'd rather eat a jar of live scorpions rather than have breakfast with my mother. My real mother. The woman who'd I'd grown up calling Mommie Dearest had turned out to be my aunt. She'd kidnapped me as an infant. Twenty seven years later she'd been murdered and suddenly I had a new mother and a huge sprawling dysfunctional family, not to mention a witch community and culture that was about as bizarre as a twelve-legged cat. Not that those exist. I think. Wouldn't bet my life on it, though.

Anyhow, now my mother wanted to get acquainted and I'd reluctantly agreed. It wasn't her fault her sister kidnapped me and then spent my entire life using me as her personal torture doll. It also wasn't her fault that she closely resembled Aunty Mommie. Nevertheless, just looking at her tended to make me first recoil and then want to kill her. At least a little.

Still, I felt a little sorry for her. She'd never had any more kids, and thanks to the birthing contract, my father had taken my two siblings (I was a triplet) and she'd never seen them again.

I made a face. Birthing contract. The witch community managed their magical bloodlines like horse breeders. They negotiated birth contracts between families, giving the studs and brood mares absolutely no say in the matter. Neither love nor lust nor like or respect entered into the equation. Basically it came down to pimping out the family chromosomes, not to mention uteruses, dicks, and vaginas.

Despite my adamant refusal to be a part of that whole baby factory thing, my father (who I'd also just met) had determined that I belonged to him and therefore would fuck whoever he wanted me to and have whatever babies he'd contracted for. Bonus—I wouldn't even have to raise them!

Excuse me while I vomit.

"Here you go, Ma'am."

The cop passed my registration and license through the window. He was an older guy, maybe around fifty, with a shaved head to cover up the fact he was bald on top. Silver threads shot through his brown mustache and goatee.

"I'm going to give you a warning this time," he said.

"Really?" I hadn't seen that coming. "Why?"

"Call it extenuating circumstances," he said without cracking a smile, but the corners of his eyes crinkled slightly.

"That's...." I shook my head. "Thanks."

"Your dog licensed?"

I frowned, shifting into momma-bear mode. "He is."

"He doesn't have a collar."

"The fuckers who had him before me kept him on a chain. When we rescued him, he was starved, covered in bruises with broken bones and his collar had worn a bloody infected trench into his neck. I won't force him to wear one again."

At my description, his face turned to granite, his upper lip curled, his nostrils flaring. "Tell me you reported the assholes."

"It was a hostage situation. You probably remember. Happened not too long ago. A month or so, maybe. Out in north of town in the hollows. Father was a mean son of a bitch who beat the wife and girls. Wife ended up shooting him and then trying to off the girls. They hid in the doghouse with this big guy."

I scratched Ajax's ears, my throat knotting with emotion. He'd been determined to protect the little girls despite being close to dead himself. He's weighed maybe fifty pounds and had broken bones from getting kicked who knows how many times. I still couldn't quite believe that Lorraine had managed to save him. "Not sure what happened to the mother. Prison I hope. No idea what happened to the girls. They weren't a lot better off than Ajax, here."

He muttered something under his breath.

"Sorry?"

He shook his head. "Do me a favor and keep it to the speed limit."

"I'll try."

He quirked an eyebrow. I shrugged.

"You try pouring a raging hot cup of coffee on your twig and berries and not stomping down on whatever pedal you've got your foot on."

The corner of his mouth lifted. "I'd just as soon take your word for it if you don't mind."

"And even if I do mind, right?"

"I like to think I'm smart enough to learn from other people's mistakes."

I tucked my registration back into my glove compartment and slid my license into my wallet. "Is this where I tell you thanks for the break and wish you a nice day?"

He stepped back and nodded. "Drive safely. I'd just as soon not see you again."

"And here I thought we were falling in love."

He smirked. "My husband would have my balls."

"My boyfriend might have something to say about it, too," I said with pretend regret.

The mention of Damon made my stomach twist. I hadn't heard from him in days and I didn't know if I should be worried about him, worried about our relationship, or if if I was being an emotional idiot. We hadn't been seeing each other long, and I didn't have any relationship experience to work from. I was totally in the dark and feeling like a fifteen year old with a crush on the high school quarterback and having a lot of what-the-fuck issues over him liking me back. Or loving me. Damon said he loved me. I was still trying to come to grips with how I felt about that and about him and now I was wondering if he really did or if he'd been having a stroke.

Definitely an emotional idiot.

Damon had been gone a couple of weeks now after receiving an emergency call. Apparently it had something to do with his family, though he hadn't given me any details. I hadn't asked.

My new cop buddy patted the top of my roof. "Have a good—" He grinned. "A better day."

"You're a surprisingly nice cop."

"That's what everybody I don't give a ticket to says." He chuckled and returned to his vehicle.

"And now on to the next disaster," I muttered as I put the car in gear. I was still driving a Highlander. Not fancy or sexy, but it carried a lot of stuff and people and I had a fluffy bed in the back for Ajax, along with a pile of old towels for when he took a dunk in the river where I generally ran, or at my secret cove.

I knew better than to even hint the universe might have another disaster in store for me, though it was inevitable.

My whole life was ruled by Murphy's Law and Mercury was in permanent retrograde while at the same time I must have busted so many mirrors in another life the bad luck had carried over to this one. At least I had managed to avoid the emergency room for awhile.

I headed back to my house to clean up. I waved to Joseph the gate guard as I drove in, circling the looped driveway and parking at the front. I drew a long breath and let it out, fortifying myself. With a silent groan, I got out.

The place looked like a French chateau with sweeping front steps and two wings angling off the man house. Stone gargoyles of various sizes perched along the roofline front and back. I scowled at them. Auntie Mommy had imprisoned them, forcing them to swear a blood bond to guard the house and property and all its denizens forever. My Uncle Mason had been able to break the spell that kept them bound in stone, except if their protection was needed. Now they stayed during the day and came alive at night. I'd promised to find a way to release them, but so far hadn't had any luck.

Actually, I hadn't tried all that hard. I'm a highly untrained witch. I have a lot of power and determination, which allows me to do a lot of stuff, but I hadn't wanted to let Auntie Mommy know I had power, so used it very sparingly. Stupid, since it turned out she knew exactly what I was, but I hadn't known that. I had no training and no clue how to begin to free the gargoyles. I'd tried, but I needed more than a seat of the pants approach. Damon had started teaching me witch language and basic spells, but then he'd left town.

Taking a deep breath, I steeled myself to go inside, my body tensing, my stomach churning. I hated it here. This is where Auntie Mommy had spent years torturing me. I'd sworn I'd never come here willingly, and now I was living here. The universe has a crappy sense of humor. A psychic had made a very vague and ominous prediction promising that trouble was coming, and then she'd written out an enormously complex spell all over the walls of Stacey's stepbrother's indoor gym. I had no idea what the spell did or why it had been so important that Lindsey had to been whipped into a frenzy to write it out. She had no idea either. Not what it meant or why.

I'd taken picture to send to Damon, but they disappeared off my camera as fast as I could take them. I'd tried copying onto paper, but it disappeared again. Then it faded off Luke's walls so that the only copy of it was seared into my brain. Nobody else who'd seen it could remember it, including Lindsey.

More than a little unnerved, I'd moved into the house. It had magical protections along with the gargoyles, though I hated the idea that they might have to protect me. I needed to find a way to free them before that became a potential issue.

I had a lot of enemies, most of whom I didn't know, and most of them wanting me for my magical DNA. Apparently I was the Serena Williams of broodmares. I came from two of the most powerful magical families of the witching world. They had an electronic server that disseminated emails to every witch, and I'd promptly sent everybody a message to fuck right off and that I wasn't interested in birthing no babies, but someone had already tried to kidnap me for my womb. He wouldn't be the last. Likely my father already had a kidnap squad or ten already planning my capture.

I had nightmares about being put in some kind of catatonic state and popping out babies two or three at a time for as long as my body held up. With magical healing, it could be a long time. Bile flooded the back of my tongue and I swallowed. It didn't matter how many times I declared I was never going to let that happen. The cold hard reality was that if someone got a hold of me, they'd give me a lobotomy and turn me into an EZ Bake oven for whoever wanted to put a bun or three inside me.

I'd tried to convince my three best friends—Stacey, Jen, and Lorraine—to move as well, but they just hugged me and assured me they weren't targets. I had to admit that while worried about them, I hated be alone in the mausoleum. Not that I was really alone. I had servants.

That fact alone was enough to make me vomit. I disliked the concept of servants. I didn't like people waiting on me and cooking for me or opening the door for me or doing my laundry. I'll admit, not having to clean the toilets or scrub the floors was nice, but I'd gladly go back to doing them for a little privacy. Unfortunately, when I'd inherited the house, I'd inherited the servants, too and I wasn't about to put any of them out of a job, so I was learning to live with having people constantly around.

I jogged up the steps and hadn't reached the top when the door opened.

"Hey, Linus," I said striding past the butler.

"I didn't expect you back so soon, Miss Beck."

"Just Beck," I said yet again. "I spilled my coffee."

"So I see."

I shot him a sideways glance, pretty sure he was laughing at me. His expression remained as bland as ever. It was a goal of mine to get him to break control and laugh.

"I hope I didn't interrupt your morning orgy."

"Not at all."

"I haven't been gone that long. You might want to get some blue pills to help your stamina."

"I'll keep that in mind for the afternoon orgy. I'll have another coffee prepared while you change."

"Thanks."

"Of course, Miss Beck."

"I know I've told you to drop the Miss thing and just call me Beck."

"Yes, Miss Beck. You have."

"And you're just going to keep doing it anyway."

"It would appear so."

"Maybe I should start calling you Mister Linus."

"That is your prerogative."

"Did you like *Aunty Mommy? Like working for her?" The questions shot out of me before I knew I was going to ask it. I'd been wondering about it since I was a kid but never wanted to chance asking in case Aunty Mommy retaliated against him or whichever servant I asked.

"One does not judge one's employer."

"Did you know what she was doing to me?" Another question I'd been holding back. I wasn't sure I wanted the answer. What would I do if he *had* known? He couldn't have done anything. Aunty Mommy would have turned him into a cockroach if she didn't kill him outright.

"It was apparent she was abusing you, yes."

I couldn't be sure, but I thought his gaze hardened with the acknowledgement.

"She hurt any of the staff?"

"No. She would not." He said it with perfect certainty.

"I suppose it's hard to get good help." Especially those who'd conveniently ignore her nasty torture habit. Resentful anger sparked in my chest. I knew what she was capable of and that crossing her was dangerous, but I couldn't help wondering what would have happened if one of the servants had called her out or reported her. Maybe she wouldn't have killed them. Maybe someone would have stepped in.

Right. Who? The only ones who could have were witches, and she'd done an excellent job of hiding from the witching world, and who knew what sorts of spells she might have used on the staff to keep them from reporting anything?

"I'd better get changed."

I heard a quiet, "Yes, Miss Beck," as I hurried off. So much for making him laugh. Maybe next I'd try talking about the Holocaust or slavery or something equally amusing.

I'd changed into another outfit and was coming back down the stairs when my phone beeped and then rang. I checked the id screen. Stacey.

I smiled. "Hey! What's going on?"

Silence.

My stomach clenched. "Stacey? Are you there? What's going on?"

A soft groan. "I may or may not have fallen and I may or may not have broken my leg. Maybe some ribs, too. Can you come take me to the hospital?"

I catapulted down the last of the stairs and sprinted for my car. "Where are you? Do you need an ambulance? Did you call 911?"

"Phone's dead. Can't call anybody but you, thanks to that little spell you put on it. Thank goodness for that or I'd be seriously fucked."

I could hear tears in her voice and the little gasps that told me she was hurting a lot worse than she was trying to let on. Plus she was talking in that peculiar voice people get when they're speaking through held breaths while keeping themselves braced against the pain.

"Where are you?"

"Well, that's part of the problem." Her laugh quickly turned into a whimper. "Ow ow ow. Fuck me that hurts."

"Where. Are. You?"

"I don't know."

"Excuse me?" My pulse had leaped into high gear. I wrenched open my door and started the engine, setting my phone down as the car picked up the signal. "Can you hear me still? I'm in the car."

"I can hear you. I took my bike out to the bluffs. Decided to do a little cross country. Hit a rock or something and took a header. Crashed into a little ravine. Crap, Beck. It hurts like a dinosaur chewed me up." She let out a short litany of curses and then went silent except for what sounded like deep breathing.

"I'm on my way," I told her, stomping on the gas pedal, my tires squealing. "Which parking lot? Did you go north or south from it?"

"Parked up by Ghost Creek Trail. Took the lower side and went off-trail maybe three or four miles in. Was trying to reach Schism Point."

Before I could respond, I heard some bumping and shuffling and then a loud clatter.

"Fuck! Beck, I dropped the phone. I can't reach it." Stacey sounded scared and close to crying.

"It's okay. I'll find you."

"Beck? I can't hear what you're saying!"

I heard sounds like the scrape of rocks and then a loud cry of pain and then crying. My hands clenched on the steering wheel and I jammed my foot to the floor. Stacey didn't cry, which meant her injuries were serious.

I wondered if I should call for help. Call the cops or the parks service. I shook my head. I wouldn't risk the connection to Stacey. Anyway, I could find her faster.

"I'm coming! Hold on, Stacey! Keep talking to me!" I shouted the words as loud as I could, negotiating a curve and nearly going up on two wheels. Times like these I really missed my Thunderbird. It cornered smooth as butter at high speed. This Highlander was more top heavy.

"I hurt, Beck. I can't... Just please get here fast. I think I'm going to pass out."

# TO MY READERS

Thank you for hanging out with me, Beck, Ajax, and the gang! If you enjoyed *Putting the Chic in Psychic*, consider leaving a review on your favorite book-buying site. Also, read excerpts from my other books on my website and sign up for my newsletter to hear more about upcoming releases at: www.dianapfrancis.com

# ABOUT THE AUTHOR

Diana Pharaoh Francis is the *USA Today* and Amazon Bestselling writer of fantastical, adventurous, and often romantic fiction. She holds a Ph.D. in Victorian literature and literary theory. She's owned by a corgi, a mini blue heeler, and a blue-eyed corgi mix. She spends much of her time gardening, airbrush painting, herding children, and avoiding housework. She likes rocks, geocaching, horses, knotting up yarn, and has a thing for 1800s England, especially the Victorians. For more about her books and to sign up for her newsletter, visit:

**www.dianapfrancis.com**

*YOU CAN ALSO FIND HER ON:*

**INSTAGRAM:**

www.instagram.com/di_pharaoh_francis/

**PATREON:**

www.patreon.com/dpfrancis

**TWITTER:**

twitter.com/dianapfrancis

**FACEBOOK:**

www.facebook.com/Diana.Pharaoh.Francis

# ACKNOWLEDGMENTS

No book is written in a vacuum. Thank goodness, because can you imagine trying to squeeze inside a Dyson every time you wanted to make words? *Putting the Chic in Psychic* was originally published as part of *Dirty Deeds II*, with works by Faith Hunter, R.J. Blain, Devon Monk, Jennifer Estep, and yours truly. My first thanks need to go to these fabulous women in helping to make that project happen.

I also need to thank the many friends who helped support me through the trials and tribulations of writing and publishing this. Without them I'd be in a padded room banging my head against the wall. So I'm raising a glass to all of you! Christy Keyes, Missy Sawmiller, Jen Stevenson, Pat Rice, Cynthia Porter, Jeff Howe, Ingrid Phippen, Barb Pollack, Jayne Fury, the writers of Authors of Urban Fantasy, and the Rainforest Writers. I also am supported by an amazing Patreon group and I want to give a special shout out to Nancy M. Tice and Barb Cass for their exceptional support.

Thank you to the fabulous writers of Book View Cafe. I'm so proud to be one of you.

I have the most amazing husband who has been my rock forever and I'm so grateful to have him. Love you, Tony. Could not do this without you. Nor could I do this without my kids—Syd and Quentin—as well as my bonus kid, Kara. I also couldn't do this without my furbabies who provide entertainment, snuggles, warmth, and love.

Finally, thank you to my readers. Thank you for loving my stories and putting your hard-earned cash down to make my dream possible. You're simply the best.

For everyone who has contributed and I forgot, my apologies. I am so grateful for everyone who has been there for me and I wish you all the very best!

# ABOUT BOOK VIEW CAFÉ

# BOOK VIEW CAFE

WWW.BOOKVIEWCAFE.COM

Book View Café is a professional authors' publishing cooperative offering DRM-free ebooks in multiple formats to readers around the world. With authors in a variety of genres including mystery, romance, fantasy, and science fiction, Book View Café has something for everyone.

Book View Café is good for readers because you can enjoy high-quality DRM-free ebooks from your favorite authors at a reasonable price.

Book View Café is good for writers because 90% of the proceeds goes directly to the book's author.

Book View Café authors include New York Times and USA Today bestsellers, Nebula, Hugo, Lambda, Chanticleer, National Reader's Choice, and Philip K. Dick Award winners, World Fantasy, Kirkus, and Rita Award nominees, and winners and nominees of many other publishing awards.

Book View Café's Newsletter includes new releases, specials, author news, and event announcements.